I0847313

Sweet Rescue

HONEYSUCKLE TEXAS ★ BOOK 8

CHRIS KENISTON

Indie House Publishing

Indie House Publishing

MORE BOOKS
By Chris Keniston

Honeysuckle Texas
Sweet Beginnings
Sweet Surprise
Sweet Temptation
Sweet Deal
Sweet Obsession
Sweet Tomorrows
Sweet Redemption
Sweet Rescue
Sweet Devotion

The Billionaire Barons of Texas
Just One Date
Just One Spark
Just One Dance
Just One Take
Just One Taste
Just One Shot
Just One Chance
Just One Mistake
Just One Family
Just One Rodeo
Just One Surprise
Just One Look

Hart Land Lakeside Inn
Heather
Lily
Violet
Iris
Hyacinth
Rose

Calytrix
Zinnia
Poppy
Picture Perfect

Farraday Country

Adam
Brooks
Connor
Declan
Ethan
Finn
Grace
Hannah
Ian
Jamison
Keeping Eileen
Loving Chloe
Morgan
Neil
Owen
Paxton
Quinn

Honeymoon Series

Honeymoon for One
Honeymoon for Three
Honeymoon for Four
Honeymoon for Five
Honeymoon for Six
Honeymoon for Seven

Aloha Romance Series:

Aloha Texas
Almost Paradise
Mai Tai Marriage
Dive Into You
Look of Love
Love by Design
Love Walks In

Shell Game
Flirting with Paradise
Fake Dating the SEAL

Surf's Up Flirts:
(Aloha Series Companions)
Shall We Dance
Love on Tap
Head Over Heels
Perfect Match
Just One Kiss
It Had to Be You
Cat's Meow

CHAPTER ONE

Josh Coleman tightened the chin strap on his tactical helmet and checked his vest seals. Temporarily based in Texas, the air felt more like an oven on Thanksgiving. Always on, always getting hotter. Sweat slid down his spine, but his focus stayed locked on the six-vehicle convoy lined up for inspection.

"Transport three's thermal reading is climbing faster than the others." Scanning the line, he clipped the handheld scanner to his tactical vest. Responsible for convoy security, these routine checks had become second nature during his years of service.

Kade Sweet, his longtime friend and the Military Working Dog handler assigned to their team, approached with Rambo, the Belgian Malinois, trotting attentively at his side. Fitted to his muscular frame, the dog's tactical vest matched their own. "All set?"

"Right about now, I'd kill for some of your mother's strawberry lemonade."

"Tell me about it." Kade chuckled. No doubt his buddy's thoughts were taking a detour to the Sweet family ranch, quiet evenings, soft breezes, and his mother's lemonade. A quick blink and he was all business again. "Rambo already cleared the first two vehicles. No alerts for explosives. What's the issue with transport three?"

"Looks like a coolant leak." Josh gestured toward the heavy truck carrying fuel reserves for the joint training exercise. "I'm not taking chances with that much combustible material on board."

As convoy security commander for this mission, Josh had final say on safety protocols. The chain of command was clear—he made the decisions, his team executed them, and everyone got home safe. The straightforward nature of this assignment should have made it routine: escort training ordnance and fuel supplies to the far range where a joint exercise was scheduled to begin tomorrow morning. Simple enough on paper.

The transport driver approached, wiping sweat from his brow. "Problem, Staff Sergeant?"

"Need to check your engine compartment." Josh's tone was professional but left no room for debate. "Pop the hood."

The driver complied, releasing the hood latch with a metallic click. Josh leaned in carefully, avoiding the scorching metal components. His training had taught him to trust his instincts, and something about this situation felt off. A small puddle of green liquid had formed beneath the radiator, and the coolant reservoir showed a hairline crack along one side.

"Losing coolant fast," Josh stepped back. "This vehicle isn't going anywhere until it's replaced." He turned to Specialist Boglioli, his communications operator. "Radio base. We need a replacement transport before we continue the mission."

"But we're already behind schedule," the driver protested. "Can't we just add more coolant and keep an eye on it?"

Josh fixed the driver with a steady gaze. "Not with what you're hauling. One spark near a fuel leak and this whole convoy lights up like the Fourth of July."

Moving closer, Kade kept Rambo on a short lead. "Listen to the man," his easy Texas drawl masked the authority in his voice. "Staff Sergeant Coleman's been running convoy security since before you could shave."

The driver's shoulders stiffened under the rebuke. "Yes, Staff Sergeant."

Josh nodded to Kade as the driver walked away. "Thanks for the backup."

"No problem." Kade crouched to check Rambo's tactical vest, adjusting a strap that had loosened. "Dog's been acting antsy since we stopped. He's flagging something."

Scanning the sparse landscape around them, Josh frowned. Training grounds stretched for miles in every direction, mostly scrubby terrain broken by the occasional patch of mesquite trees and dirt roads. Nothing but heat waves shimmered on the horizon. "Think the heat's getting to Rambo?"

Kade shook his head. "He's desert-trained. This is nothing for him." He gave a quick hand signal toward the front of the line. Rambo trotting beside him, he called over his shoulder, "I'll finish clearing the lead trucks."

Josh waved acknowledgment, turning his attention back to the idling transports. They hadn't gone ten yards when Rambo suddenly stopped mid-stride, muscles going rigid, his head snapping back toward the rear of the convoy. A low growl rumbled from deep in his chest, sharp and warning.

Frozen in place, Kade's hand hovered near his sidearm. "What is it, boy?" He followed the dog's focus toward the fuel trucks behind them.

Josh's pulse spiked. Rambo wasn't one to false-alert— something back there wasn't right.

The radio on Josh's shoulder crackled to life followed by Boglioli's raspy voice. "Base confirms replacement transport ETA forty minutes, Staff Sergeant."

"Roger that." Josh's attention remained fixed on Rambo's behavior. By detecting threats before human senses could, military working dogs had saved their lives more than once during previous deployments. Josh would trust a well-trained K9 before humans any day of the week. Something sharp and chemical tainted the air—too faint for his nose, but dogs didn't false-flag.

"Check the rear vehicles again. Full inspection."

"On it." Kade nodded, already moving with Rambo toward the back of the convoy.

Josh followed, signaling for two more team members, Hanson and Gideon, to join them. If Rambo sensed something was wrong, there was a reason. Whatever was going on up front wasn't what had Rambo spooked. Different truck, different threat.

They approached the rear transport—another fuel truck—where Rambo's behavior intensified. The dog strained against his lead, hackles raised, growling more loudly now.

"Something's definitely got him worked up." Kade's voice dropped to a near whisper as he maintained control of his partner.

Josh gestured for the driver to step away from the vehicle. "When's the last time you checked your engine temperature?"

"Just before we left base, Staff Sergeant. Everything was normal."

About to take a reading, Josh reached for his scanner when a sharp metallic crack echoed from somewhere beneath the truck. The sound wasn't loud—barely audible over the idling engines—but Josh's combat-honed instincts registered it instantly. It wasn't a mechanical pop; that hollow metallic snap had the signature of something man-made under tension, about to give. Adrenaline shot through his system. "Clear the area!" Moving at full speed, he waved his arms, directing his team to a safe distance. "Everybody back now!"

The world seemed to turn in slow motion. Josh sprinted toward the front of the convoy, shouting orders as he moved. "Boglioli! Get the lead vehicles moving!"

Having just finished checking the forward vehicles, Kade and Rambo were again at the front of the convoy. Josh could see him turning at the commotion.

"Possible detonation! Clear out!" Josh bellowed, urging nearby soldiers to move faster. Two men were still too close to the suspect vehicle, frozen in momentary confusion. Damn it. He changed direction, rushing toward them. "Move!" Josh shoved the nearest soldier forward.

The blast hit before he cleared the path, followed instantly by another detonation. The shockwave caught Josh and the two soldiers in the open, lifting them off their feet. He felt himself hurled through the air, a blinding flash searing his vision as the pounding force crushed against his chest, slamming him to the ground. Beside him Hanson wasn't moving and Gideon lay several feet away, unnaturally still. Josh's chest burned and his side screamed.

Through the ringing in his ears, he caught a flash of Kade dragging Rambo behind the lead truck—both safe. Relief flickered, even as darkness closed in.

His only clear thought—what an unholy mess.

Thumbing through the last pages of her mystery novel, Katie Lawford confirmed her guess halfway through the book had been accurate. No point in finishing it now. One week into the government shutdown, and she'd already cleaned out her closet, labeled her spice jars, put dividers in her junk drawer, binged two seasons of a show she'd been meaning to watch for ages, and finished three books from her "to-be-read" pile.

She glanced at her phone. No alerts, no panicked emails from her supervisor, no updates about when the Department of Defense contract administrators might return to work. Just silence and the ticking of her grandmother's antique clock. "So much for those *urgent* military supply contracts," she muttered, stretching her legs on the couch. The unexpected furlough had been nice—at first. But now, a week later, restlessness was settling in.

Her phone buzzed. *Finally.* She snatched it up. "You rescued me from organizing the freezer."

Jackie Sweet's laugh came through bright and familiar. "Tell me you're not still cleaning. It's a furlough, not a punishment."

"It's both." Katie dropped onto the sofa. "I've rearranged every shelf I own. Even the ones that don't need rearranging."

"We can't have that." There was a long pause. "So, tell me. How are you doing really? I mean, do you need money or something?"

Oh, how she loved her bestie. She couldn't help but smile. "I'm fine. I have a very understanding landlady. Mrs. O'Grady has been through this before. Whenever the government shuts down, lots of Houston contractors wind up at home sitting on their hands with no paychecks. She knows we'll get paid eventually, so she's told me it's all right to hold off on rent until I get a paycheck. Even though I have a good nest egg just in case."

"Well, that's a start."

Another long pause and Katie knew Jackie was stewing on something. "Might as well spit it out."

"Why don't you come ride this shutdown out here? It's been ages and we'd all love to have you."

"Oh, sure. You and Garret are still technically newlyweds. I bet he wants a fifth wheel tagging along about as much as he wants to step on a rusty nail—barefoot."

"Don't be silly. Garret loves having you around as much as I do."

"Uh huh."

"Really. You know what this house is like. Organized chaos with a double dose of love and laughter."

Her friend had a point. She'd only spent a few days at the ranch for Jackie and Garret's wedding, and there was never a moment when anyone was alone, and that seemed just fine with everyone. Heck, half the siblings were still living at the house and they were all newlyweds.

"Carson and Jess' new place is really taking shape. They put the sheetrock up this last week and it's actually looking like a house and not so much like a kid's construction toy."

"I bet they can hardly wait." She remembered the talk about starting building as soon as some of the family business was taken care of. Mason, their son, was the most excited about having his own house while torn about leaving his Nonnie alone in the Main house. It was kind of cute.

"Now, if you want to be helpful, the guest annex is down to the cosmetic stages. Alice picked out the paint colors the other day. Mostly soft beiges and yellows."

"Yellow?" She couldn't picture Alice Sweet picking out yellows for that big old western style home.

"I think she calls it warm butter." Jackie chuckled. "The funny thing, she looked at something ivory for the bathroom and to me that thing looked like French mustard. No idea where these companies get their color names from."

"You don't want my opinion. Last time I helped you paint, your living room wall looked like a bad Picasso."

"That's only because you grabbed the wrong paint can."

"It said living room."

"And here we go again. *Trim.* It said living room trim." Jackie's laughter now was a far cry from the horror on her face when she walked into the room and found her camel walls blotched with patches of not quite white over every filled nail hole.

"A very valid reason why I should never be given a paint brush."

"Okay. No painting," Jackie's voice still held a healthy dose of humor. "But seriously, when's the last time you had a vacation? And I don't mean time off to clean out your closet or catch up on your laundry. A real get out of town vacation?"

"I get out of town."

"I don't mean for weddings."

Well, that poked a hole in her argument. "Touché."

"Does that mean you'll come out and visit?"

"What if Congress stops the pissing match and we all have to go back to work?"

"Then you go home, but when have you ever known a shutdown to last only a week?"

Point to Jackie. "Let me think about it."

"Don't think. Pack."

Had her friend always been this pushy? Her mind turned to when Jackie gave up everything to chase after the wrong man. Yep, she'd always been this pushy. "I'll think about it."

"Well," Jackie sighed, "I guess I'll have to settle for that. For now."

Setting her phone on the side table, Katie looked

around. She really did love her little garage apartment. Nestled in the Memorial neighborhood of downtown Houston, there were mature trees lining every street, lots of colorful blooms, well manicured lawns, and no cookie cutter homes—yet. This apartment had lots of character, and she liked that. Her gaze landed on her dwindling pile of books to read. It was time to face facts; she was bored out of her mind. But West Texas?

Once more she took in her surroundings. Before she realized what she was doing, she found herself in her room, yanking her suitcase out of the closet. "West Texas, here I come."

CHAPTER TWO

Staring up at the ceiling, Josh bit down on his back teeth. Every time someone bumped against his bed he felt like he was riding out a tsunami in a rubber raft. It had been days since the explosion and he still couldn't catch his balance. At least not one hundred percent of the time—and you didn't serve in Uncle Sam's army if you were less than one hundred percent.

A small part of him muttered in the back of his mind to stop bitchin'. Of all the guys who'd been caught in the blast, his vestibular dysfunction was the least serious injury. Even the gash in his side no longer bothered him. On the other hand, his buddies were going to be stuck here for a while, and it was still a coin toss if Kent was going to make it out of the burn ward at all.

"What are you still doing in bed?" Kade appeared at his bedside. "Didn't you get the memo? You're being discharged today."

He would have nodded, but that would bring on the nausea.

"You packed?" Kade glanced around.

Reaching slowly, Josh used the control to lift the head of the bed and gingerly inched himself to an upright position. "Not much to pack. Nurse helped."

"The pretty one?" Kade teased.

That made Josh smile. "Which one?"

"Damn." Kade shook his head. "I've only seen the brunette. There are more?"

He heaved a deep sigh, not from frustration but more of a wowza response. "Red hair, green eyes, and an hourglass would wither beside her."

"If I weren't a happily married man, I might be tempted to request you stay longer so I can get a glimpse."

While he would be the first to agree that the nurses here were definitely easy on the eyes, he was ready to get out of this place. What he wasn't looking forward to was convalescing. No one would tell him how long it would be before this stupid inner ear thing would go away. Or if it would ever go away.

Not till this moment did Josh realize his buddy was out of uniform. "Did the brass give you the day off to be my chauffeur?"

"Nope. Gave me the whole week." Kade waved the orderly over to the bedside. "Your getaway ride has arrived."

Very slowly, he eased off the bed and managed to sink into the wheelchair without getting dizzy. If it wasn't progress, he was willing to pretend that it was. "You need a week to drive me to housing?"

A grin took over Kade's face. "No housing."

His brows pulled up on his forehead. "What do you mean no housing? They can't kick me out."

"Not out. Doctors say you need to have someone around to keep an eye on you."

He huffed—okay, maybe it was more of a grunt. At least it wasn't a growl. "I haven't needed a babysitter since I was five."

"Good, because you're not getting a babysitter."

"All right. You do realize, even for you, you're speaking in riddles. Just get to the point."

Kade heaved a deep sigh. "Well, I wasn't going to tell you till we were on the road and too late for you to object, but we're heading to the ranch. My mother is expecting you so you can't refuse."

Of course he could. A bigger part of him did not want to be on the receiving end of anyone's pity. He could dang well go to his army housing and lick his wounds in private. Though he had to admit, he'd taken a real liking to the Sweet family ranch, and the Sweet family. Kade might just have a point. Fresh air, peace and quiet, and down home cooking would probably go a lot further to improving his physical condition than sulking in a recliner in front of the boob tube.

"I'm going to take your silence to mean you agree."

Before he could say a word, Kade and the orderly were walking side by side talking about small town Texas as if it were a Hawaiian paradise. Friendly people, pleasant weather, blue skies, chicken fried steak, and sunsets as far as your eyes could see. He couldn't disagree with any of it, which was probably why he hadn't made any formal objections when Kade announced his plans without consulting him.

Next thing he knew, his bag was in the trunk of Kade's rental, he was strapped into the passenger seat and the lousy headache he'd had for almost a week was actually fading without meds. Maybe that was a good sign. "You sure your mom doesn't mind?"

"You're kidding, right?" Kade shot a sideways glance in Josh's direction. "You're lucky she didn't show up days ago to make sure you're being well cared for. If I had let you go home she'd be yanking on my ear."

"Your ear?"

"Yeah. If we dared step even slightly out of line, which trust me was not often, she would grab us by the ear and drag us to face my father."

"Wow. She seems so nice."

"She is nice, she just didn't want to raise a bunch of hoodlums. Besides, Dad was more of a pussycat. He would put on a good show for Mom but he would always take it easy on us."

"Obviously that worked."

"Mostly because we were warned, if we didn't toe the line, he'd throw us back to our mother."

That had Josh laughing out loud for the first time since the convoy exploded. After his time with Mrs. Sweet, he could see why no one would want to cross the line. Good thing he wasn't a wayward teen.

Katie had no idea if she had ever slept so soundly in her life. A city girl, she'd never given any thought to what it might be like to live out in the middle of nowhere. And West Texas was filled with a lot of nowhere. Driving across the state, she was honestly shocked when she reached the massive expanse of land with little more than an occasional cluster of cows huddled under the lone tree or shade canopy. By the time she'd reached the Sweet Ranch, she was flabbergasted by the panorama. The sun wasn't quite setting and the sky was painted with startling shades of reds, oranges, and bright pink that would have made any artist proud.

Even though the land seemed to go on forever with little more than varying shades of yellow, it was truly breathtaking. She'd barely pulled into the front yard when Mrs. Sweet—Alice—came hurrying down the front steps to greet her with the same enthusiasm as a parent embracing their prodigal child. Anyone would think that Alice Sweet had known Katie her entire life and not just since Jackie's wedding.

Dinner had been chaotic, hectic and the most fun she'd had since the last time she'd come to Honeysuckle. By the time everyone had excused themselves to head to their own homes, Jackie and Alice had escorted her upstairs to Jillian's old room.

"You planning on sleeping all day?" Jackie tapped lightly on the bedroom door before nudging it open and popping her head inside.

Stretching like a lazy cat awakened from an afternoon of slumber, Katie smiled at her friend. "Debating how awful would it be to spend my vacation on this bed. Is this a feather mattress?"

Jackie entered the room fully and crossed to sit at the end of the bed. "I think it's just a feather topper. But it's heavenly, isn't it?"

Yawning, Katie nodded. "I really should get up."

"Alice is making her famous French toast casserole. You'll want to get it while it's hot."

"Does it come with coffee?"

Jackie laughed. "By the gallon."

"Then I'm in." She flung the blankets off the bed and swung her legs over the side. Twenty minutes later she was showered, dressed, and stepping into the kitchen. "Oh man. It smells amazing in here."

"Thank you." Alice pointed to the table with her nose where Jackie was already cradling a warm coffee.

Katie poured herself a cup and settled into a seat beside her best friend since college.

With a spatula in her hand, Alice scooped out a hefty portion of the breakfast casserole, added a few strips of bacon and set the plate in front of Katie. "I hope you were comfortable last night?"

"Very." She took her first sip of coffee. Heaven.

"I know we thought you'd be able to use the new guest suite but Kade has a buddy who will be staying here while he recovers from an accident and Kade said going up and down stairs wouldn't be advisable."

"Oh, my." Katie set her mug down. "Of course I don't mind. That room upstairs is perfect and probably the most comfortable bed I've ever slept in, but I do hope it's not serious. Kade's friend."

Alice shrugged. "Not sure yet what we're getting into. Kade was pretty tight lipped."

No sooner had the words left Alice Sweet's lips than the sound of a car door slamming, followed shortly by another, echoed through the house.

Her head lifting, her gaze riveted to the front door, a smile to outdo a kid on Christmas morning took over Alice Sweet's face. After only a few minutes, the smile was replaced by a frown and Alice crossed the room quickly, swinging the door open and pretty much marching out onto the front porch. Her jaw dropped slightly open, ready to say something, and then sighing heavily, she snapped her mouth shut, her gaze fixed on something in the distance.

Suddenly feeling in the way, Katie decided to find something to make herself useful in the kitchen. Something she couldn't muck up. Glancing around, she wondered how the Sweet matriarch would feel about her sweeping the floor? Surely that couldn't be a problem. Everyone likes help cleaning house—didn't they?

Only halfway to the kitchen, the back door swung open and Cassie appeared, stomping mud off her boots. "Are they here? Thought I heard a car pull up."

"It seems so."

Cassie practically flew past her to the front door making Katie wonder how long had it been since she'd seen her husband. Next thing to cross her mind was wouldn't it be nice to feel that way about someone. She was still standing in the middle of the hall daydreaming about the perfect love when she spotted Alice Sweet slowly making her way up the porch steps, her arms open wide as if ready to catch a flying football. The sight was odd enough to have Katie inching forward herself. Not toward the kitchen but toward the front of the house.

Alice led the way back to the house. Cassie walked at her husband's side, tucked under his arm.

"You're doing great," Alice encouraged the man walking behind her.

"Mom," Kade almost whined from behind his friend, "he's not a toddler learning to walk. He's fine."

"I really am, ma'am." That voice washed over Katie like a warm blanket on a winter's night. She stood rooted to the floor, curious to see if the man matched the voice.

Another moment and Alice hurried inside, a tall sandy blond man with broad shoulders and twinkling eyes crossed the threshold. If this was the wounded buddy, he looked awfully healthy to Katie. If she were honest, he looked absolutely delicious.

"Take a seat. Make yourself comfortable." Alice waved to the living room sofa. "You'll be inaugurating the guest wing. Kade will get your things."

"Thank you, but I can grab my bag." His head whipped around to point at the front doorway when all of a sudden, his eyes went wide, his arms sprung out sideways and he wobbled like one of those children's toys that wobbled but didn't fall down. Until he did. On her.

CHAPTER THREE

What a way to make an entrance. Not only did Josh lose his balance—again, but like a line of dominoes, he fell on the woman standing in the hall, who fell on Alice, who landed on Brady. The dog had magically appeared out of nowhere as if he knew Alice would need a soft landing because Josh was going to make an idiot of himself and fall after only minutes in the house.

"Oh my."

He wasn't sure which woman had said that, but Josh did his best to raise himself before he completely crushed everyone beneath him. If only the stars dancing before his eyes would go away.

"Easy." Kade's fingers curled around his arms, easing him upright.

"Never mind me." Very, very slowly, he turned his head to see Alice and another woman lifting themselves up from the floor with Jackie and Cassie hovering over them.

"Anyone going to check on Brady?" Josh was teasing, but the way Alice's eyes flew open wide and she spun around, almost losing her own balance, to check on the retired K9, he wished he hadn't been so cavalier. "I'm sorry about that. Is everyone all right?"

Alice Sweet actually laughed. "Hate to break it to you, but you don't weigh near as much as a steer. Now those suckers really do damage when they slam you against the fence, or God forbid, stomp on your feet."

"No ma'am. I don't believe I do." Relief made breathing easier, though he still felt ten times the fool for having forgotten not to move so fast and falling on these nice ladies.

"I guess I should ask." Alice eyed him from head to toe. "Are you all right?"

"I'll be better when my inner ear stops throwing me off balance. I really am sorry."

"Nonsense. Like I said, I've had worse happen to me."

His gaze shifted to the other woman he'd fallen into. "I do apologize."

"Not your fault. Besides, every woman dreams of being swept off her feet some day." The pretty blonde smiled. "This just wasn't exactly what I'd had in mind."

So the woman had a good sense of humor. Thank heaven. He was embarrassed enough. It would only have been a hundred times worse if he'd actually hurt anyone, or if this woman had thrown a fit. Instead, for the first time since the explosion, he actually felt like smiling back. "I'll try and do better next time."

The lovely shade of pink that tinged her cheeks broadened his smile.

"I should probably introduce you two officially." Alice waved from him to the blonde. "Katie Lawford, Jackie's maid of honor and longtime friend, this is Josh Coleman, Kade's longtime buddy."

Katie extended her hand to him. "Nice to meet you."

As long as he didn't move his head too fast, all was well with the world, especially with a sight like Katie Lawford. "The pleasure is all mine."

"Okay." Alice slapped her hands together. "Now that we have the formalities out of the way, let's get you settled into the guest suite and then we'll work on feeding you."

The women all turned and made their way to the kitchen, but Kade lingered a moment, placing his hand on Josh's shoulder. "You all right, man?"

"You mean other than embarrassed to no end? Fed up with losing my balance so easily? Refusing to consider that this may be my lot for the rest of my life? I'm fine, thanks for asking."

Kade's brows shot up high, creasing his forehead before settling back to their designated place over his eyes. "Well, as long as you're good." He slapped Josh on the back and forced a smile.

"Sorry. I told myself I wouldn't throw a self-pity party."

"Everyone's allowed to blow off steam. Let's follow the ladies. Whatever Mom's cooking is bound to make you feel better."

Walking slower than he wanted to, by the time he'd made it into the kitchen, Kade had jaunted back to the car, retrieved their bags, and walked past him into the kitchen and down a side hall.

"You go ahead and follow Kade. I'll have a warm plate for you in a few minutes."

Josh came within seconds of nodding when he remembered that would not be a good idea. Not unless he wanted to do a face plant in the kitchen. Instead, he smiled and proceeded down the hall. The setup was rather simple. A large open space to the right and another to the left. Next room on the left was clearly intended to be a small kitchen area. Cabinets and appliances had yet to be installed, but he recognized the placements for pipes. At the end of the hall was the last room. This room was finished. The walls were painted a warm buttery beige, the trim a not too bright white. A queen bed with small dressers at either side faced a large screen TV on the opposite wall. Beside the table and nightstand was a comfortable leather recliner with a view out the window facing a large expanse of Sweet land. Not a bad way to wake up in the morning. At the foot of the bed was a large upholstered bench with his travel bag resting on top.

"Bathroom is this way." Kade pointed to the doorway. "The family rushed to get this part habitable."

"For me?" That didn't sit well, putting the family out to cater to his health issues.

"Not exactly."

"What exactly?"

"Mom wanted it ready for Katie, but then I said we were coming and she shifted the bedspreads to be more suitable for a male guest."

His gaze wandered back to the bed. He hadn't even noticed that it was a deep chocolate brown with tan Euro pillows perfect for reading that matched the recliner, and a couple of blue smaller pillows for a pop of color. Definitely not a girly bedroom décor. "So, what you're saying is I kicked her out?"

Kade shook his head. "She never moved in. She only arrived last night and Mom put her in Jillian's old room." Before Josh could say a word, Kade kept talking. "And stop frowning. Jillian's room is very nice. I'm sure Katie is perfectly comfortable. Besides, the last time she visited for Garret and Jackie's wedding, she stayed upstairs and didn't have a single complaint. I don't think she even knew that the guest annex was being built."

All right. Maybe he hadn't put the pretty blonde out on the street. So why did he feel like he'd just stolen candy from a baby?

It took everything in Katie not to keep looking over her shoulder for Kade's friend. There was something about that man that felt irresistibly magnetic. It occurred to her that not having a man pressed up against her, even by accident, in a very long time might have something to do with her keen interest, but the truth was, had Kade been the one to fall on top of her, she would be laughing it off right now.

She couldn't put her finger on it. Yes, the man was drop dead gorgeous with deep set eyes, high cheekbones, a five o'clock shadow worthy of a magazine cover and muscles that could probably crush nutshells with his bare hands, but there were lots of good looking, strong men in this world. None had her so sucked in only a few minutes after being introduced that she was almost oblivious to everything else around her.

Not wanting to be caught peeking at the doorway, she'd just shifted her seat at the table and did her best to focus on the food on her plate when the two men returned to the kitchen. Kade took a seat beside his wife, the two smiling at each other like a couple of smitten teens. Josh sat across from Kade, beside Jackie. As Alice scooped out warm casserole for Josh, Sara Sue came through the back door. "Morning."

"Just in time for a late breakfast." Alice smiled.

The way Sara Sue grinned, Katie got the impression that was exactly what Alice's first daughter-in-law was hoping for.

"There's eggs too." Alice spun around holding a large frying pan with one hand and a serving spoon with the other. "Who wants some?"

Every voice at the table spoke up with a resounding *me*.

Moving about like someone perfectly at home in the kitchen, Sara Sue grabbed another bottle of juice from the fridge, and with her free hand transferred the platter of bacon from the counter to the table. "One of these days I'm going to figure out how you get the bacon just right every time."

"Wait till you're my age, you'll have perfected the art of bacon too." Alice took a seat between Jackie and Sara Sue. "Not that I'm complaining, but what brings you by this morning?"

"Well," Sara set her fork back on her dish, "I need a little help."

Alice nodded in silence.

"I've got a dog that is recovering from a shrapnel wound after a convoy explosion."

Casting the occasional glance in Josh's direction, Katie noticed an almost imperceptible tightening of his jaw at Sara Sue's comment. She had an inexplicable urge to reach out and pat his hand or brush his shoulder. Instead she stabbed at her food and considered sitting on her free hand.

"The wound was healing fine, but his behavior indicates that he's most likely also depressed."

Again, Katie spotted Josh's response, his finger tightening around the fork. Again she refrained from reacting.

"We've tried a couple of foster homes, but the dog was not bonding. Last placement, he tore at his sutures and set his recovery back."

Alice leaned back, a concerned frown giving way to a

knowing smile. "So we get him."

"If you're still interested in fostering."

"You know I am."

For the next few minutes Sara updated her mother-in-law on the dog. Another German Shepherd, closing in on retirement age but who still had some work left in him before this incident. Apparently, he saved several soldiers by alerting to the situation before the firestorm. Poor dog had lost quite a bit of weight between the recovery from surgery and loss of appetite.

"If he can't thrive here, I don't know where he will." Sara Sue sighed.

Alice reached across the table and squeezed her daughter-in-law's hand. "Don't you worry. If we can't figure out how to help him, Brady will."

Katie followed Alice's gaze toward the dog sprawled out on the floor, looking totally relaxed, until upon further observation a person could see he was actually focused on the door. More than focused, he was strategically resting between his people and any potential danger coming through that door. Smart dog.

"When can we expect him?" Alice reached for her cup of coffee.

"As soon as I can arrange transport." Sara Sue's gaze darted over to Kade and smiled. "An experienced handler would help."

Fork in hand, Kade returned the smile. "As long as it's before I have to report back for duty, you've got yourself a handler."

"Good." Sara Sue pushed to her feet, lifted the plate of untouched food. "I need to go make some phone calls. The sooner I get Raider here the better." She turned to Alice. "Mind if I take this with me?"

Alice waved to the other side of the house. "Why don't you use Charlie's office. At least the food won't get cold heading back to your cottage."

"That would be great."

"If you need a ranch vehicle, I'm sure something can be arranged."

Sara Sue stopped short, set the plate back on the table, and threw her arms around Alice. "I love you. Thank you."

Alice's face lit up before all expression washed away and she patted her daughter-in-law's back and made a shooing motion toward the front hall. "Go. The sooner you make those calls the sooner we can settle Raider in."

And just like that, conversation shifted to ranch business, family updates, and a sprinkle of oohing and aahing over the delicious food. This family seemed to be a Norman Rockwell painting come to life. No wonder Jackie loved life here at the ranch. Fresh air, Mother Nature at her best, supportive family, good looking men—heck, if Josh were a Sweet and needed to marry to save the ranch, she suddenly understood how Jackie had so easily married a perfect stranger. As surprising as it was, she could see herself agreeing to a marriage of convenience with Josh in a heartbeat. Maybe it was something in the water?

CHAPTER FOUR

I f Josh thought the morning at the Sweets had been busy and bustling, there was no comparison to dinner. He had no idea if the entire family showed up for him, for Katie, or just because they were hungry.

Either way, Alice's dining table looked like a recruiting poster for Happily Ever After, Sweet Edition. Plates, platters, and bowls covered every inch of wood. Conversation bounced from one end of the table to the other like a well-served ping-pong ball.

"Pass the potatoes before Kade eats them all," Jackie ordered.

Flashing a toothy grin, Kade reached for the bowl. "I'm carb-loading,"

"Pretty sure you have to do cardio for that to count." Garret returned the stupid grin.

"Says the guy who spent all day sitting at a desk." Kade pointed his fork down the table. "We chased a stray bull for two hours this morning."

"First of all," Garret waved a finger at his big brother, "I'll trade chasing bulls to keeping a class of middle schoolers in line any day of the week."

"Would this be a good time to mention that we chased that bull on horseback?" Clint reached for the green beans.

The siblings teased over who worked the hardest and who had the life of Riley. All the while laughter rolled around the table. And Josh thought, not for the first time, no wonder Kade was so well adjusted. Lots of guys had their issues and egos, but Kade was a solid soldier. He and his K9 partners through the years had saved a whole lot of lives, but no one who wasn't there would have any way of knowing by simply hanging out with the guy.

"You doing okay over there?" Alice's voice broke through, soft but direct. "Getting enough to eat?"

Josh glanced down at his plate. Chicken-fried steak, potatoes, gravy, green beans, a biscuit the size of his palm. "Yes, ma'am. I'm trying to pace myself so I don't embarrass my entire unit."

"Too late, he already face-planted in the hallway." Kade turned to Katie. "Our other guest broke his fall."

Katie nearly choked on her water.

Anyone else, and Josh would have had a colorful retort; instead, he plastered on a smile. "I'll be performing nightly."

The room filled with more chuckles and laughs, but Alice was the one to shake her head. "Please don't. I'm not sure Brady's up to it."

"Sorry, ma'am." He could have hurt someone the way he collapsed. His gaze drifted to where Katie sat, thankful he hadn't hurt her, thinking how nice it might have been to find himself in her arms for a completely different reason than he couldn't keep his balance.

Alice Sweet smiled and reached across the table to pat his hand. "I'm only joking. You can fall on all of us anytime you want."

Sitting up straight, Brady let out a deep bark before rocking his head. Whether it was an agree or disagree, Josh wasn't sure, but he was very sure that all of this was why bringing him here to heal might very well be the best idea Kade ever had.

"So." Leaning over to scratch at Brady's scruff, Alice turned to Sara Sue. "What's the status with Raider?"

Josh's fork slowed. He wasn't sure why his pulse kicked up at the dog's name, but there it was.

Sara Sue set down her fork and nodded. "As I expected, you've been approved to foster."

"Good." Alice's whole expression softened.

"Raider's six years old."

"So he would have had at least two more years of service." Josh remembered what she'd said earlier in the day about his not being ready to retire except for the injury. He could certainly relate. "Or as much as six."

"Exactly," Sara Sue agreed. "He's been deployed three times. Mostly convoy and route security, some gate work. Solid nose, good nerves. Until the last mission."

"Well trained," Kade muttered under his breath.

Josh wasn't a handler, but he'd been around the dogs and their human partners enough to have learned a good deal. That diversity of assignments meant someone had a treasured K9. "What about his handler?"

Sara Sue huffed. "Depends who you ask."

That didn't sit well with Josh. He knew how hard losing a K9 partner hit a soldier. He'd seen good men go into depression, PTSD, lose their edge. Others got right back into the thick of it with a new dog, but none ever stopped worrying about their former partners.

"He checks in on Raider as often as he can. Psych eval says he's ready to get back in the thick of things. His CO says the relationship isn't there yet. He's not sure that the handler isn't masking his own issues."

Nodding his head, Kade tsked. "It's like having a brother your whole life, then one day the brother has to go away and a new guy shows up and says he's your brother now. Your dog is not a favorite toy, he or she is family."

Katie's gaze flicked quickly to Josh, then away. He'd done his best not to think about the explosion that he knew had injured the dog in the first place. Not think about how he too was sent to the Sweets to heal. Not show signs of how unsettled the unknown was for him. Much like Raider, he had no idea if he'd ever be able to go back to work or if he'd be on the sidelines for the rest of his life. And he had no idea if Katie was somehow reading all of that or if she'd just happened to glance his way. Another place, another time.

"Same for the dogs." Sara bobbed her head. "They don't understand what has happened to their humans."

"Poor baby," Alice spoke softly.

Yeah, and Josh knew exactly how that poor baby felt.

Katie couldn't help but notice the tension in Josh's shoulders. Every so often, he seemed to squeeze his fork more tightly. Sometimes, he'd watch the folks around the table, and then other times, he'd look down at his plate as if interacting with humans was painful.

"Because of the recent issue with his wound re-opening," Sara Sue continued, "he needs to be assisted outdoors with a belly band."

"We can do that." Alice reached for the basket of biscuits.

"There are plenty of us around to help," Carson added while beside him his wife bobbed her head.

"Exactly. Not only do y'all have plenty of hands-on help, tending to injured animals is nothing new to anyone around here and the cherry on top is that y'all understand working dogs, both ranch and military." A smile spread across Sara Sue's lips. "And of course, you have the added asset of a retired military dog to help show Raider the way."

Under the table, Brady thumped his tail once, as if he knew he'd been volunteered.

Josh cleared his throat. "Any anxiety meds?"

"Not yet," Sara Sue replied. "We're hoping if he comes here, we won't have to."

Everyone at the table was keenly aware of the situation with the injured dog and eager to help, but she wondered if anyone had noticed Josh's reactions to the situation, or was she the only one worried about him? Which made no sense, she'd barely met the man.

"So now what?" Alice asked.

"We transport him."

"We?" Clint spoke up.

Sara Sue's gaze darted to Kade. "We move dogs about all the time, but I've convinced the vet that having an experienced handler would be an asset if we can get the paperwork done before you return to base."

"I can tag along, but I should not be the one to work

with him. He needs to bond with people who are going to be caring for him."

"That would be me." Alice raised a finger.

"And me," Clint added and Katie's heart shifted at the precious way that Alice smiled over at the man in her life.

The muscle in Josh's jaw began to pulse. She could almost see him grinding his teeth as he worked something over in his mind. Setting down his fork, Josh looked up at his buddy. "I'd like to tag along too."

Kade eyed his friend a long moment before finally nodding.

That settled, the conversation shifted to other things, mostly around ranch business, an occasional mention of a unique customer at the candle store, or the challenges with Carson's latest projects.

Having grown up an only child, all this teasing and laughing and general shenanigans was out of the norm for her. She'd obviously had friends with siblings, but none with this many. Even though she'd been exposed to all of them at Jackie's wedding, everyone had been more focused on their tasks for the big reception. Tonight, things were much more low-key, and Katie found herself enjoying it even more than her last visit—despite her concerns for the Sweet's other houseguest.

After supper, everyone moved around the kitchen and dining room, clearing plates, wiping tables, rinsing dishes, storing leftovers. The typical after dinner chores only multiplied on a larger scale for a gathering that would rival many dinner parties in size. The kitchen nearly sparkling, the siblings who lived outside the main house, one by one, kissed their mother and made their way to their own homes. Carson and Jess were upstairs reading to Mason; Katie had learned last night that this was a ritual that could often last an hour or more as they worked their way through another Louis L'Amour book. Kade and Cassie had wandered out to the barn to check on a new foal. It was Katie's understanding that Cassie had grown up in the city but had taken to ranch life like a pig to mud.

Finishing up drying a few stray pots and pans, she

noticed Josh walking very slowly toward the back door. His hands not quite extending, but not quite at his sides, no doubt trying to keep his balance.

"Why don't you go relax on the back porch. I'll make a nice pot of tea." Alice turned off the water faucet.

"Oh." Katie set the dry pan in the cabinet below and set the towel on the counter. "I can do that."

Drying her hands, Alice shook her head. "No need. Go."

At that moment, Clint turned from the fridge where he'd stored the last of the leftovers and smiled at Alice. Everyone in this place was insanely happy and it showed. Except for Josh.

Her gaze drifted to the back door, excusing herself, she made her way outside. Closing the door behind her, she carefully strolled over to where Josh sat on the swing. "I love swings."

He lifted his gaze to follow the chains that hooked into the ceiling. "I suspect there have been a lot of nights spent stargazing and snuggling on this thing."

"I won't argue with you." Not wanting to invade his space, ignoring a ridiculous urge to test out the snuggling idea, but more curious if he was all right, she leaned against the railing and stared out into the distance. "Hard to believe Honeysuckle and Houston are both in Texas. So different."

"Ranch country is different from most places on the planet."

"Do you think that Raider will really be okay here?"

He took so long to respond that she turned to face him. He was staring into the distance, eyes narrowed. "It might be hard for him at first. Being a service K9 is probably all he's ever known." He remained quiet another few seconds. "I joined up right out of high school. The army is the only life I've ever known."

"So you know how Raider feels?" She didn't want to mention the explosion was another thing they had in common.

He nodded. "I think if this place can't heal him, no place will."

Tempted to ask more, she sensed now might be too soon, too raw. Instead, she walked closer to the swing and leaned back against the railing again. "Won't it be difficult switching handlers?"

"Not all dogs spend their entire careers with one handler."

"I see." She glanced over her shoulder and then back again. "I thought every handler had his own commands, his own demeanor, making it hard for someone else to work with their dog."

"Some. But most commands are standard, like sit, stay, down, drop it, guard or stand down. Enough that working with the dog shouldn't be hard. Now, bonding, that's a whole other issue."

"Mm," she murmured. "Do you think I can come along for the ride?" She had no idea where that request had come from, but now that the words were out, she knew that she'd meant them. She wanted to see this dog, and maybe, if she could, help. Not that she had any idea how. "I'd stay out of the way."

He shrugged. "It's not up to me. I suspect it might not even be up to Sara Sue. The decision may very well rest in the hands of the clinic that has Raider in its care."

"I suppose." Now she did glance away, returning her attention to the stars splattered above.

"It's pretty amazing, isn't it?"

Whirling around, she leveled her gaze with his. A question in her eyes.

"The stars," he explained, before a little smile tugged at one corner of his mouth, "and for what it's worth, I think Raider would be a lost cause if he didn't find you a pleasant addition to his recovery entourage."

"Thank you for that." She knew her cheeks had to be flushing bright red at the compliment. What she didn't know was if he was really speaking for Raider, or for himself?

CHAPTER FIVE

The sun shining through the window meant Josh had slept longer than he should have. This family was up and about before sunrise seven days a week. Since he couldn't really do much with physical labor, he didn't see any real reason for climbing out of bed and rushing to dress and leave his room. Besides, he was enjoying replaying last night on the porch with Katie.

There was nothing spectacular about the quiet evening. Nothing earth shattering or mind boggling. Except for the blanket of stars, that was pretty impressive—as was the company. What made the time together even nicer was that for the first time in weeks, he felt almost…normal. Katie didn't treat him like someone who needed to be coddled or pitied; she just hung out, as if they were friends. And right about now, a friend seemed like a really nice perk. Though he knew she could be called back to work any day, the idea of having her around actually made him smile. And wasn't that an interesting twist of fate. His usual response to a night out with a pleasant female was more like Mark Twain's views on company: after three days it starts to stink. In Josh's case it was more like after three dates. He couldn't remember when he'd actually looked forward to spending more time with a woman, especially fully clothed.

A rap on the door dragged him away from the memories of the porch and back to his room.

"You up yet?" Kade's voice carried easily through the door.

"Yeah. Come on in." He didn't bother to sit up. If he moved too quickly, that could bring on a dizzy spell and he was getting seriously fed up with them. If he eased up slowly, then he'd be showing his weakness. Not that it mattered in front of Kade, there were no pretenses, but his pride just wouldn't let him.

"Listen, I heard from Sara Sue. There are a couple of trauma cases coming in to the veterinary facility and they can't keep Raider. We're leaving to pick him up in thirty minutes if you still want to tag along."

"Absolutely. I'll be ready."

Once the door latched shut, Josh eased himself up, slowly swung his legs over the side and taking a couple of minutes to make sure he wasn't going to tip over, proceeded to stand. Feeling almost proud that he was still on solid ground, he went ahead and showered and dressed and took his meds. The doctor had said these pills could work in as little as a few days or as much as a few weeks. So far a few days didn't seem to be the answer; if he was still wobbly after a couple of weeks, they'd regroup. He wasn't going to let himself go down that path, wondering what if this would become the standard for the rest of his life—today he had a dog to help rescue.

Dressed and in the kitchen, the house seemed oddly quiet.

"Mom's working with Clint on the never ending repair of fence lines." Kade came in the back door. "I've got the Suburban set up. Lots of blankets and pillows."

"Pillows?" The blankets made sense, but pillows?

"Yes. Lots of dogs enjoy a good pillow, just like people."

"You're kidding?"

"I am not."

"I've never seen a K9 using a pillow."

"Give me a break." Kade rolled his eyes. "Where we usually are, the men don't even get pillows!"

"Point taken." He turned slowly, stiffly, looking for Katie.

"She's already in the truck." Kade waved a thumb over his shoulder toward the back door.

"Who is?"

"Katie. Isn't that who you're looking for?"

Sometimes having a buddy who could read your mind was a real pain in the backside. A lifesaver when deployed on a less than easy mission, but a real pain when you don't want someone to know what you're up to. "Sara Sue."

Kade stared for a minute as though ready to call his bluff and then gave a quick bob of his head. "We'll pick her up."

Following his buddy, when they reached the SUV, Katie was already in the back seat.

"Sara Sue will ride shotgun. She knows where we're going. You ride with Katie."

He almost nodded and then quickly caught himself. "10-4." The challenge now was to climb in without triggering a dizzy spell but still looking totally normal and at ease. Grabbing onto the handle, he put one foot on the running board and taking special care not to look down or move his head much, he swung himself into the seat, more than a little delighted that he didn't sway or keel over.

"Good morning," Katie spoke softly.

Again, he almost nodded, but instead simply smiled. "Morning."

"Sleep well?"

"Very." Great. Single word answers. Anyone would think they had only just met, in a bar, under awkward circumstances. And even then he could usually come up with a suave line that would have the ladies eating out of his hand... so to speak. Leaving him tongue tied was not something he'd experienced, even as a hormonally driven teen.

Thankfully, his momentary lack of eloquence didn't seem to bother Katie as her smile reached her eyes. "I don't know if it's the air, the house, the food, or the mattress, but I have never slept as well as I do here."

"I know what you mean. I felt the same way when I visited a few months ago, and if last night is any example, I'm going to continue to sleep like the proverbial baby." He just hoped whatever magical powers the ranch held over sleep bled over into restoration of an inner ear.

In the front seat, Kade and Sara Sue chatted about the

dog. Raider was stable enough to move but from what Sara Sue said, he was uncooperative. More so than when they'd released him the previous time.

"I'm not sure if the foster couple were simply in over their heads with his medical needs and temperament, or if they did something to aggravate the situation." Sara Sue frowned and Josh wondered if she'd already decided on an answer.

"Won't be too hard to tell. Military dogs are extremely well trained. Even injured, they have certain instincts and responses. I might be able to draw a few conclusions once I see him face to face."

Sara Sue smiled. "I was hoping you'd say that."

The drive didn't take long. The veterinary facility was larger than Josh had expected. He had no idea why he'd assumed that being so far out in cattle country surrounded by mostly small towns that didn't even qualify as cities, that it would mean a veterinary clinic would be small scale. What was the old saying: Everything's bigger in Texas. Certainly applied to this place.

Inside the building, most of the staff seemed to already know Sara Sue, no surprise there since rehoming former service dogs was what she did for a living. He suspected most of the folks at Lackland where the military dogs came through probably knew her as well.

"He's in back." An older woman with a smile that reminded him of Aunt Bee from the old *Andy Griffith* television show tipped her head toward a corridor.

The three of them followed Sara Sue down a long hall and around a corner to a large kenneled area. No one needed to tell him which dog was Raider. In one of the few large kennels, lying on his good side, a stunning German Shepherd zeroed in on them as they entered. The animal was very obviously sizing them up, and when Sara Sue softly called his name, and the animal lifted his lip exposing rather large white teeth in response, followed by a deep, low growl, Josh was pretty sure the animal had made up his mind. And he didn't think any of them was going to like Raider's conclusion.

Katie couldn't help herself. The minute Raider snarled at Sara Sue, she found herself taking a step back and slipping behind Josh.

"Better let me." Kade came out in front of Sara Sue. "If he had a bad experience with the fosters he may blame you."

It was obvious by the tight press of her lips that the idea didn't sit well with Preston's wife, but she nodded and circled behind him.

"Easy boy." Kade barely moved, his voice soft and low and with only two words, almost mesmerizing. "I bet it's hard being in there, isn't it fella?"

The dog didn't cease to show his teeth and if anything, the growl seemed to rise in volume.

Kade crouched down to his level. "I promise, things will get better, Raider."

At the use of his name, the dog's ears seemed to twitch and his growl appeared to dim, but those big old fangs were still staring the three of them in the face.

"We've come to take you to a really happy place," Kade continued.

Kade's words brought the dog's growl back and Kade heaved a deep sigh.

"This," Kade slowly pushed to his feet, "is not going to be easy. He doesn't like you, and I'm not winning any brownie points either."

"So now what do we do?" Josh asked.

The three were talking, but Katie couldn't take her eyes off the dog. The funny thing; while the three of them were discussing possible sedation for transport, she noticed something unusual. "Uh, excuse me."

Kade turned first. "Yes?"

"Look." Very carefully, she gestured with a finger toward the dog.

The three of them turned to face the animal.

"Hmm," Kade grunted.

"What?" Josh asked.

"He seems to be watching…you."

"And he's not snarling," Katie added.

Very slowly, maybe even slower than usual, Josh turned to fully face the dog and took a long step to the side, away from the group.

As expected, the dog's eyes remained fixed on Josh, his teeth no longer exposed.

"I'll be." Kade narrowed his gaze in thought. "Try talking to him. Low and soft."

"I know." Josh took a single step closer to the dog. "I remember." Crouching in place, he continued speaking slow, soft words of reassurance.

The dog heaved a sigh and Katie wondered what hold Josh had over him. Did he somehow remind the dog of his former handler? Or a special person? Or did the dog just know that he was a good person? But that made no sense. She knew Kade was a good person and the dog wasn't having any of it.

His fingertips splayed on the floor beside him, Josh inched closer. "It's no fun being hurt, is it?"

Raider shifted ever so slightly, almost as if trying to stand despite his injured leg and hip, his focus never leaving Josh.

"I bet about now you probably need to go outside, don't you?"

Now the dog tried to push up in earnest.

"Whoa." Josh lifted one hand straight out, his wrist flipped and his palm exposed with fingers tightly together, the other still on the floor keeping him balanced. "Stay."

To her surprise, the dog did just that. He seemed to freeze in place.

Slowly, Josh turned his head toward Kade. "Is this medically all right?"

One of the techs came forward. "It probably is time for him to get a bathroom break and it's good for him to get a little exercise, but…" the woman twisted in place and retrieved a large canvas band from the wall, "he'll need some help. It's too soon to put all his weight on that leg."

"I'm guessing he's not very strong yet, either." Eyes closed, Josh sucked in an audible breath and pushed himself upright. When he opened his eyes she thought she saw a flash of surprise. "I'll take that."

"Good idea," the tech said. "He hasn't been very happy with any of us and he seems to like you."

Silently, Kade and Sara Sue bobbed their heads in agreement. Kade carefully watched man and dog, no doubt looking for any sign of trouble coming.

With measured movements, Josh carefully unpinned the gate to the kennel and coaxed Raider to come forward. Another couple of minutes and the dog was leashed with Josh holding the belly band under him for extra support. Like a parade, the three of them and the tech followed Josh and the dog through the nearby door to an open grass area.

Josh continued to murmur to the dog, almost like a man whispering endearments to a woman.

All of them kept their distance, keeping an eye on the pair, hoping that the connection between man and dog would last. But Katie was the only one who seemed to be in awe. The extreme gentleness that Josh displayed with the injured dog was nothing she'd ever seen before, except maybe from a nurturing mom. The guy was so tall, and strong, and muscular, and, well, handsome—not that handsome had anything to do with anything. From what she understood, he was a military man, a warrior. And yet, the man was so tender, she couldn't help but think she would very much like to know more about the real Josh Coleman. For the first time since the stupid shutdown started, she hoped the politicians would take a good long time to settle their disagreements.

CHAPTER SIX

Josh had no idea what was going on, but helping this service dog relax and lose some of his fear was the most useful he had felt since the day the convoy exploded.

He was just about to turn Raider around to return inside when the vet tech called out, "That's probably enough. He needs to build his strength slowly."

Just as he had thought. With a nod, Josh and Raider inched their way back inside and to the kennel. Unlike before, the towels and blankets were gone, and a canvas fabric with long poles at the sides, rested on the ground. Tired from his few minutes outdoors, Raider barely sniffed the fabric before pretty much collapsing in place.

"Now what?" Josh stood at the front of the kennel and faced the tech.

"Now," the woman smiled, "you take him home. Is your vehicle ready?"

Kade nodded. "I'll take one side of the stretcher."

It took a second, but Sara Sue jumped in, moving forward beside Kade. "I'll take the other side."

Everything in him wanted to say, *no, I'll do it*. But the risk of moving too fast, or too clumsily, and losing his grip on the handles and dropping the dog, was too great. There was nothing about having Sara Sue step in that sat well with him. As careful as he had been with his steps and efforts, and as good as he seemed to feel today, all it could take was one wrong turn and it would be over. It simply made sense for someone else to help Kade. Still, Josh didn't have to like it.

"What can I do?" Katie looked to the adults gathered by

the kennel.

"I guess," Sara Sue looked up from where she stood near Kade watching Raider, "get the door for us and be ready if we need a hand." Without hesitation, she turned to Josh. "You too, but stick close, Raider may need to hear your voice once we start moving him or jostling him into the Suburban."

He nodded. At least, though it was a crumb, having a job made him feel a fraction less useless.

Even though Kade was speaking softly to Raider, the moment he and Sara Sue approached him, despite clearly being exhausted from his brief effort outside, the dog lifted his lip and snarled.

"Okay." Kade blew out a sigh. "Looks like you're going to have to come close now and reassure our future houseguest so he doesn't literally bite our heads off."

Without nodding, he eased his way up to the dog and since he couldn't lean over without risking imbalance, he carefully squatted. "I bet you're tired."

The dog's upper lip stopped twitching, though his teeth were still very visible.

"I get that way too. Especially now. Just sitting around doing nothing seems to make me more tired than when I was up at the crack of dawn and going all day."

Raider's lip fell, covering all his teeth. Good sign.

Josh took a chance and extended his hand in front of the dog. It took a long minute before the dog diverted his gaze from Josh's face to his hand. Another few seconds and the dog gave him a long lick, then another. When Josh looked up, all three faces were grinning at him.

"Let him know we're going to try again," Kade urged.

"These nice people are my friends." Josh moved his hand as he spoke, taking a chance on touching the sweet boy. "I'd appreciate it if you wouldn't bite them." The dog huffed what sounded an awful lot like a resigned sigh. Daring to scratch the scruff of the dog's neck, Josh was delighted when the dog seemed to lean his head into Josh's palm. "I'd say we're good to go."

Grabbing onto the side of the kennel, Josh carefully

eased himself to an upright position as Kade and Sara Sue lifted the dog. The interesting thing was, the dog never looked at anyone but Josh. He didn't look at Kade or Sara Sue, or anyone else inside the busy clinic. The dog leveled his gaze with Josh's and kept it there as if his life depended on it.

Not till he felt the weight of the dog's head against his hand did Josh realize he'd been scratching the dog's neck the entire walk to the Suburban.

Katie hurried in front of them, quickly opening the rear doors of the SUV. At this particular moment, Josh was very thankful that this model didn't have a hatch door but two doors that swung open. This allowed them more room to maneuver the dog into the back. Staying as close to Raider as he possibly could without getting in the way, he locked his gaze with the dog's and watched his friends settle the animal onto a comfy blanket.

All set to step aside and join Katie in the back seat, Josh stopped short at the pressure on his arm. Still gazing at him, Raider lifted his front paw and almost seemed to be grabbing Josh, pleading for him not to move.

"Well, I'll be." Kade ran his hand across the back of his neck. "I haven't a clue what it is, but this dog really likes you."

"What do you mean you don't know what it is?" Josh put his hand to his chest as though the comment were an affront to his character. "I'm a very lovable person."

Kade burst out laughing. "As long as Raider thinks so."

"Comedian." Josh shook his head. "I'm going to ride in back with him."

Kade shrugged and Katie opened her mouth as if about to say something and then snapping it shut again, seemed to change her mind.

Hanging on to the side, Josh sat at the back then lifted his legs up and inside. He hadn't dared crawl up and in the way he might have only a month ago. The moving might have upset his equilibrium, or lack thereof. Thankfully, he wasn't any taller or he'd have had to duck while seated inside. Making himself at home beside the dog, he continued to scratch him, all the while hoping the drive home went by faster than the ride into town.

Katie couldn't help but keep looking over her shoulder at Josh and Raider. The dog seemed to be perfectly still and actually looked comfortable. Josh was slightly hunched over the dog, scratching its neck and murmuring soft words she couldn't quite hear. Whatever he was saying seemed to do the trick as the dog kept his eyes closed.

When they finally rode over the cattle guards under the gateway to the ranch, Josh had stopped talking, but the dog appeared to still be sleeping.

"We probably need to rethink our plans." Kade eased his foot off the gas and Katie wondered which part of the plan he was talking about.

"Raider?" Sara Sue shifted in her seat to see behind her.

Kade nodded. "I know we initially thought the calving barn would be the best place for him to recover, but I'm not so sure."

Now Josh lifted his head and looked to the front seats. "I could stay with him. Your new barn has plenty of space for man and beast. Just leave me a sleeping bag and we're good to go."

"This isn't Kabul." Kade rolled his eyes. "If you need to stay with him, there's no reason you can't stay in your own bed. But that is sort of what I'm thinking."

"In my room?" Josh asked.

"Yeah." Kade nodded. "The floors in the guest wing are vinyl so that's good for any accidents. There's a private entrance so it won't be a long walk to get Raider in and out to relieve himself."

"And keeping him calm will help him heal faster," Josh added.

"And," Katie jumped in, "stop him from ripping out his stitches again."

"Exactly," Josh said.

"Then we're all agreed?" Kade glanced up at the rearview mirror to see his passengers.

"The question is how will your mom feel?" Josh continued to stroke the sleeping dog.

"Delighted to have someone else to fuss over. That dog is about to become very spoiled." Kade flashed a grin at everyone.

Josh suddenly frowned. "What about Brady?"

"Good question." Kade sighed.

"I think," Sara Sue turned to face them again, "Brady will be fine with Raider. He's proven to be a good K9 mentor with Samson. How Raider will react to Brady is another story."

"Guess we'll find out soon enough." Sara Sue pointed to the front porch where Alice stood waiting with Brady faithfully at her side.

Doors opened and the three adults in the seats hopped out. Kade made his way around to the back and opened the doors.

Katie stood at Kade's side, eager to help, though she didn't have a clue how. Watching the continued tenderness with which Josh treated the dog, a complete antithesis to the image of big bad soldier armed to the hilt and ready to fight the world, had her feeling safe and warm all over even though none of that attention was directed at her.

Easing back from petting the injured dog, Josh stared at him a moment before deciding he wasn't going to wake up quickly and scooted away from the pup until his legs hung over the tailgate. His feet dangling, Josh took a deep breath and hanging on to the side, slid out of the truck and onto his feet.

If anyone asked Katie, she'd say the man looked surprised to notice he was standing firmly on his own two feet. She sure hoped that meant he was getting better.

Alice slowly approached. "How'd it go?"

"So far so good." Josh smiled at his hostess.

Brady moved closer to the vehicle, one paw lifted high as his nose twitched with interest. Raider was still sleeping, so much so that Katie wondered if the vets had given him something for the ride after all. Brady sniffed at what he could reach of Raider. A back paw, a front paw, the tip of his tail, then Brady lifted his head and sniffed the air inside the Suburban before taking a step back and sitting at Alice's side.

All the adults were standing perfectly still, watching the family dog, Kade's former military K9, sniff and evaluate his new charge. The dog seemed to bob his head at Alice's side, as if he understood his new mission. Help this dog heal.

"Okay." Kade stepped forward. "Let's get this show on the road." He turned to his mother. "We're going to take Raider into the house."

"My room," Josh added.

"Is that all right with you?" Kade asked his mother.

"You know it is. Whatever is best for this boy."

With a nod, Kade grabbed hold of two corners of the blanket under the dog and tugged just enough for Sara Sue to grab the other corners. As they tugged a little more, the dog lifted his head, gave a low growl, but as soon as Josh spoke to him, the dog stopped.

Balancing the dog in the blanket swing, the two walked briskly into the house.

Alice was already rushing ahead. "I'll get a small mattress from the storage room."

Katie felt like a third wheel. Everyone seemed to have a purpose, except her. She wasn't quite sure what to do, but she wanted to stay close, so she continued to follow behind them. They were barely inside when Alice rushed across the kitchen dragging what looked like a mattress for a camping cot. From where she stood, she looked over to them. "Katie, would you be a dear and run to the barn a minute. Ask Benny for the dog bowls we left for Raider."

"Yes, ma'am." Delighted to feel useful, she dashed to the barn, found Benny, and a minute later was hurrying back to the house.

No surprise, Alice was scurrying about gathering old linens and towels for the dog.

"Where shall I put these?" Katie asked.

"At the head of the bed," Sara Sue responded. "This way he won't have to go far if he's hungry or thirsty."

Gingerly walking around the people standing back, she inched closer, nibbling on her lower lip. She'd seen the dog's sharp teeth and didn't want to do anything to raise his hackles again.

"It's okay, boy," Josh's voice was soft and soothing. "She's a friend."

The dog's eyes tracked her every step. Swallowing hard, she forced herself to put one foot in front of the other. She was setting bowls down for a hurt and frightened animal, she wasn't walking the plank. Too bad her stomach didn't quite believe it and continued to roll and pitch with every nervous step.

She was only a few inches away from the dog when its lips began to twitch, causing her to slow her steps.

"It's okay, Raider. All is well."

The dog stopped twitching and laid his head back down on the bed, his nose hanging off the edge.

Katie managed to breathe more easily. Squatting, she set the two bowls at the side of the bed. Before she could ease away, the dog stuck out his tongue and caught the back of her hand. Not in a vicious bite, but in a slow lick. The rough sensation along the back of her hand almost had her toppling over from the surprise.

"At least we know one thing." Josh smiled at her. "The dog has good taste."

CHAPTER SEVEN

Rising gently from the easy chair, Josh checked on Raider before leaving the room. Stretched out on his side the shepherd breathed steady and easy, sleeping peacefully. Able to leave the animal alone for longer periods of time, Josh padded softly across the room. The moment he opened the door, the tantalizing aroma of coffee and something sweet struck him. Alice. That woman was always baking something, making it very difficult to think about someday leaving the ranch and returning to army food.

Carefully pulling the door shut, eager to find out what had his stomach rumbling, he spun around a bit faster than he probably should have. The floor gave a little wobble under his feet. Not a bad one. Not enough to knock him sideways. Just enough to remind him life wasn't quite done messing with his balance. Just to be sure, he walked the short distance, one hand brushing the wall.

At the counter, Alice stood slicing a loaf of fresh bread. Cassie sprang from her seat and opening the fridge door, emerged with not one but two sticks of butter in her hand and a grin that shouted heaven was before them. Sleeves rolled up his forearms and jeans already dusty from early morning chores, Kade leaned against the doorway with a mug of coffee in his hands, smiling appreciatively at his wife for reasons that most likely had nothing to do with his mother's bread or the butter in Cassie's hands.

A warm chuckle escaped Alice as she slid another loaf onto the cutting board. "You'd think I never feed that girl."

"Fresh bread makes everything better." Cassie shrugged, her smile intact. "Broken hearts, flat tires, government shutdowns."

"Inner ear trouble?" Josh offered, stepping fully into the kitchen.

Cassie pointed a butter knife at him. "Especially inner ear trouble."

Stealing a slice of freshly sliced bread, Kade kissed his mother on the cheek. "If you ever stop baking, half this family will collapse."

"Half?" Alice sniffed. "Try all of you."

Josh eased into a chair, doing his best to look like getting there was effortless and not the careful, deliberate process that had become his new normal. "If bread counts as medicine, I'm willing to double my dosage."

"Sit." Alice slid a plate in front of him. "You need it. You're looking peaky."

Shaking his head at his mother, Kade rolled his eyes and walked to the table, taking a seat beside his wife.

Josh loved the way the Sweets interacted, how there was no telling who was kin and who was married-in. Or for that matter, that they had all started out as a marriage plot to save the ranch and found themselves truly happily married. Taking his first bite, the bread melted on his tongue, warm and soft and just the right amount of sweet. If he weren't in mixed company, he might have moaned.

Across the table, Katie breezed in with her hair pulled up in a way that made Josh momentarily forget how breathing worked. She paused, then inhaled dramatically. "Besides smelling absolutely heavenly, all this delicious baking is enough to make a girl rethink living in a big city."

That brought a good chuckle from Alice. "If only I could solve our political troubles with a few loaves of fresh bread or a good blueberry pie."

Familiar with the kitchen and fitting in as if she'd always been part of the Sweet family morning routine, Katie poured a cup of coffee and to his surprise, instead of taking a seat herself, she slid the warm mug in front of him. "Black, right?"

He nodded. Oddly content that she'd noticed how he drank his coffee.

Settling into the chair across from him, Katie blew into her mug before leveling her gaze with his. "How is Raider doing today?"

"So far so good. He's sleeping better than he's slept since we brought him home." His mind wandered back to earlier in the morning, when he'd taken Raider out for a potty break. Even though the dog was improving, watching him struggle to stand had been hard. The way his back legs trembled, the effort it took just to push himself up from the mattress. There had to be a better way. He needed to call the base hospital and check on his men. By his calculations, Boglioli should be getting his walking papers soon. Assuming his rehab was going well.

Alice settled into her chair at the head of the table, coffee in hand. "You're frowning. Something hurting? Is the dog too much for you?"

"No." Josh shook his head. "I'm fine." If he didn't consider feeling like the ground was undulating beneath his feet. "Thinking about my men and how Raider's having a hard time getting up and down. The mattress is low, and every time he tries to stand, he's straining those back legs."

Everyone at the table nodded. Narrowing his eyes in thought, Kade pressed his lips together before bobbing his head. "How about an elevated bed?"

Josh waved a finger at his buddy. "Yes. So he can just step on and off instead of pushing himself up from the floor."

"Elevated?" Katie frowned seconds before her eyes opened wide. "Oh, you mean like a hammock or trampoline."

"Exactly." Josh grinned at her. "It would be easier on his back than a mattress as well."

"Makes sense." Alice sipped her coffee. "We don't have anything like that here. I'm sure Clint or Benny could build something but I bet the feed store in town might have something like you want in stock. They carry more than just feed and tack nowadays."

Katie set down her mug. "What about his food and water bowls?"

All eyes turned to her.

"I noticed when I was setting them down," Katie continued, "Raider has to bend pretty far to reach them. He sort of braces himself every time, like it pulls at something."

She was right. The woman was pretty and smart. Another reason she seemed to be making herself at home in his thoughts. Josh had been so focused on the standing problem that he'd missed it completely. "An elevated feeder. Or a dispenser that sits higher."

"Might make eating and drinking easier on him." Katie took a sip of her coffee, eyeing him over the mug's rim.

"Sounds like a trip into town is in order." Josh turned to Alice. "Would you mind if I borrowed a vehicle?"

"Of course not."

"We could all go." Kade suggested. "A little change of scenery."

"Great idea." Alice nodded. "I can keep an eye on Raider. He doesn't love me like the two of you, but he doesn't snarl at me like he does at my son."

"Thanks," Kade huffed.

Kade's pouty face almost had Josh chuckling out loud. It had to be hard on his friend, with all his training, not being able to win Raider over. Of course, if the dog had chosen Josh over Kade, maybe all that proved was that the animal was a lousy judge of who was the better man.

The drive into Honeysuckle didn't take long. Main Street appeared like something out of a postcard—tidy storefronts, flower pots overflowing with color, and hand-painted signs advertising everything from candles to corn hole supplies. Katie had driven through on her way to the ranch, but she hadn't really seen it. Not like this. She leaned forward between the front seats. "Is it always this busy?"

Cassie laughed. "Oh no. We forgot."

"Forgot what?" Josh asked.

"Sidewalk sale." Kade pulled into a parking spot near the feed store. "First Saturday of the month during warm weather seasons. The whole county comes around."

"Jackie is going to be really mad we let her sleep in." Cassie sighed. "She loves the Saturday sales."

Sure enough, the sidewalks were lined with tables and racks. Shop owners stood in doorways waving at passersby. A group of small children chased each other around a row of display tables while their mothers shopped. Fun for all ages, she thought.

"This is amazing." Katie stepped out of the Suburban, taking it all in. A woman in a bedazzled denim jacket caught her eye—she sparkled so much in the sunlight that Katie had to squint.

"Mildred McEntire," Cassie whispered, appearing at her side. "Bling queen of West Texas."

"Unofficially," Kade added.

"Is there an official one?" Katie asked.

"Lord, I hope not." Cassie linked her arm through Katie's. "Come on. Let's get the dog stuff first, then we can browse."

The bell over the feed-store door gave a cheerful jingle the moment Katie stepped inside. The place was much larger than the modest storefront implied. Shelves stacked with feed bags, rows of colorful halters, giant tubs of horse treats, and a whole wall of tools she couldn't name, ran front to back and occasionally side to side. If they didn't have a dog bed it might very well be the only thing they didn't have in stock.

"Okay," she glanced around, this time less awed and more focused, "if I were a dog bed, elevated bowls, something soft for his head, and maybe a toy, where would I be?"

Josh muffled a laugh. "Most of the home pet supplies seem to be down that aisle, but Raider's not himself yet. He may not be ready for toys."

A voice carrying a hint of amusement, called from behind them. "Every dog's interested in toys. And the dog beds are in aisle four, the toys in five."

Thanking the clerk, they walked deeper into the store, stopping in front of a whole display of raised dog beds—mesh hammocks stretched over sturdy frames.

Josh ran a hand along one. "Yeah. This looks right."

"It's firm but springy," Katie said, pressing the center. "Like orthopedic…but cooler."

Josh gave her a look. A hint of surprise that seemed to shift to… was that admiration? Either way, being the focus of his attention had heat climbing her neck and probably turning the tips of her ears red. Instinctively, she reached behind her neck and tugged her hair loose over her ears.

They picked one with reinforced corners and an extra-soft removable pad. The kind that whispered: *injured military hero dog deserves luxury.* Next stop was bowls. Elevated, stainless steel, adjustable height. That done, they grabbed a tug toy—thick rope with knots on either end, "for gentle play only," per the tag.

Katie imagined Raider slowly reclaiming his dog joy, step by step. She liked the idea. With the supplies secured, the four of them wandered onto Main Street. The sidewalk sale was in full swing—tables piled with marked-down merchandise, racks of clothing, bins of odds and ends. Katie found herself drawn to a display of handmade jewelry outside a shop she didn't recognize.

"See something you like?" Josh appeared beside her, moving carefully through the crowd.

She held up a bracelet—simple leather cord with a small silver charm. "It's silly."

"What's the charm?"

"A star." She set it back down. "I've always had a thing for stars. Used to drive my parents crazy, begging to stay up late to watch meteor showers."

Josh picked up the bracelet and turned it over in his hand. Before she could protest, he'd caught the attention of the woman behind the table and handed over a few bills.

"You didn't have to do that."

"I know." He held out the bracelet. "I wanted to."

She let him fasten it around her wrist, his fingers warm and steady against her skin. Every time she looked at this she knew it would remind her of that night on the porch. "Thank you."

"You're welcome."

A few storefronts down, Cassie waved them over to a table piled with kitchen gadgets. "Look at this! A pickle picker!"

"A what?" Kade squinted at the contraption in her hand.

"It picks pickles out of the jar. No more fishing around with a fork."

"Who needs that?"

"Everyone needs that." Cassie added it to the small pile she'd already accumulated.

Strolling along, looking at all the items rather than where she was walking, Katie drifted a little too close to a display table and Josh instinctively reached for her elbow to steer her around it. She shouldn't have enjoyed that as much as she did. Then she spotted a booth selling custom leather dog collars with names burned into the strap. "Josh. Look."

His gaze followed hers, nodding, he smiled. "Perfect."

Raider's new collar in hand, she fell into step beside Josh, continuing down the sidewalk. A corn hole demonstration had drawn a crowd near the park. The unofficial bling queen was moving about as if she were a contestant in a world pageant. A few feet away, a lemonade stand covered in bright yellow and pink streamers drew a good crowd.

"Want some?" Josh nodded toward the stand.

"Absolutely."

They stood in the shade, sipping cold lemonade and watching the chaos unfold around them. Katie had never felt so content. Whether it was the town, the sunny day, the collar for Raider, or the man sipping lemonade beside her, she didn't know, but she was sure of one thing. She'd known plenty of nice guys through the years, but none had made a simple day of shopping feel so…special. Not for all the tea in China would she trade today, here, with Josh.

CHAPTER EIGHT

In just a couple of hours since they'd brought the elevated bed back from the store, Raider clearly loved it. He'd actually gotten off it with more ease than Josh had expected, or anyone else for that matter. Raider had gotten a sip of water from the new bowls and then lifted his nose to sniff the air, his gaze settling on Josh. He'd have sworn the dog was telling him thank you before he turned and stepped back onto the bed.

"Looks like a happy boy now." Katie stood in the doorway, watching the now sleeping dog.

Josh stood slowly and smiled. Not till recently did he realize how often he'd nodded. Something he wasn't sure he'd ever be able to do again. "He appears to be less stiff. Not sure if it's the bed or if he's just healing that quickly."

"Maybe a little of both." She shrugged. "Rachel just blew into the kitchen."

Josh couldn't hold back the burst of laughter at the comment. From what he knew of Rachel, that girl buzzed in and out of a lot of situations and then sped away with the agility of a formula one race car driver.

"Apparently, Jillian needs something and we've all been summoned."

With a shrug, he waved one hand toward the door. "Lead the way."

In the kitchen, several family members were seated around the table while Alice walked about filling glasses with iced tea.

"So what's going on?" Kade asked.

His brows buckled and his gaze narrowed, Garret tipped his head slightly. "Is Jillian all right? Did something happen at the sale today?"

That last line had everyone sitting taller in their seats, their casual smiles slipping.

"Relax." Rachel held up her hands. "You know how Jillian has decided to do evening classes on candle making?"

Jackie nodded. "She said it would be easier without customers coming and going."

"She's been leaving flyers all over town," Cassie added. "Thought the crowds from the sidewalk sale would be good timing."

"Makes sense." Preston nodded.

"So what's this all about?" Leave it to Kade to get right to the point.

"She's only had two people sign up. A couple staying at the new B&B."

"Hm." Carson grunted softly. "Even for me, that math doesn't add up."

"Nope." Rachel shook her head from left to right once. "If she wants this to catch on like that painting and wine event that folks are always doing, she'll need more people and more making merry along with the candles."

And the reason for the meeting became clear to Josh at about the same time it hit everyone else and several heads either nodded or turned side to side.

"I love my sister," Carson spoke, "you know I do, but tonight is Mason's last parent night at school."

Jackie looked at Garret. Their eyes met. And Josh wondered how the heck did these people do that? He could see the entire conversation taking place without a word, then Jackie turned to Rachel. "We're in."

A smile took over Rachel's face. "Who else?"

One by one hands went up. Before he knew it Cassie was nodding and Kade was elbowing him. "Come on, hot shot. Afraid a little candle making will tarnish your reputation with the ladies?"

Hot shot? That was a first. He'd let the ladies comment ride—for now. On the other hand... "No more afraid of word getting back to the men on base than you are."

Kade winced and Josh understood his pain. If word spread that the two of them were spending a Saturday night making candles, they'd never hear the end of it for the next ten or twenty years.

"So," Josh looked to Kade, "is there a dress code for this little party?"

And just like that, voices spoke over each other, laughter floated around and then, beaming like the Cheshire cat, Alice placed the handset to the landline back in place and spun about. "Aunts Liz and Vicki are going to come too. They were going to watch the competitions at the park, but agreed this is more important." The woman slapped her hands together and rubbed. Still grinning madly, she actually squealed before spinning around. "This is going to be so much fun!"

He sure hoped Alice Sweet knew of what she spoke.

"Hey," Cassie grabbed her husband's hand, "don't look so grim. This will be a great date night. Certainly better than sitting in a dark theater watching a dumb movie."

Wise man that he was, Kade merely smiled at his wife and nodded.

Something deep inside Josh seemed to almost tug at him to turn and face Katie, surprised to find her hands cradling her glass, her gaze focusing on the liquid within. Not till he spotted the hint of pink warming her cheeks, did he realize what had made her so quiet. The same words that had struck him—*Date night.* Great, so the woman was not only smart and perceptive, she was also cute as a button when she blushed. Maybe a date night wouldn't be such a bad idea.

If there was one thing Katie had learned during her short visits at the Sweet ranch, it was when this family mobilized, it was like watching a well-oiled machine. Within half an hour, everyone was changed, freshened up, loaded with bottles of wine, and good humor. Shortly after leaving the ranch, the siblings, spouses and friends piled out of various vehicles in front of Jillian's candle shop as if it were the hottest ticket in town.

Katie carried a massive bottle of red wine that Jackie had pressed into her hands with the fierce conviction of a woman about to commit mischief.

Heaven Scent had been transformed. The overhead lights had been dimmed in favor of string lights that gave the whole place a cozy, almost magical glow. Near the rear of the shop six workstations had been set up, each equipped with a hot plate, a double boiler setup, measuring cups, wooden stir sticks, and an array of small glass jars. And wine—lots of wine.

Katie took it all in, handing Jillian the bottle of wine that had been clutched to her chest. Not that from the look of the table set up for refreshments did it seem that Jillian needed more. "This is adorable."

"Right?" Jillian beamed. "I was panicking when only two people signed up, but now—" she gestured to the growing crowd, "—now it's a party."

Josh followed behind her, moving a little slower but his broad smile had his eyes twinkling with amusement. Looking around a minute, he stepped around her and reached for two aprons from the counter, his other hand brushing along the small of her back. The unexpected contact had her sucking in a long breath. Turning, he offered her a colorful apron with the candle shop logo. "Here you go."

"Thanks," she managed, slipping it over her head.

Behind them, two women who Katie remembered from the wedding as being Garret's Aunts Liz and Vicki came through the front door, both smiling and giddy as schoolgirls going to their first dance. Within minutes, wine glasses in hand, they settled at a table, whispering and laughing and reminding Katie, in the words of Auntie Mame, that life was a banquet and most poor suckers were starving to death.

All the couples claimed a table leaving Josh and Katie at the same table. Her thoughts drifted back to Cassie's comment about a fun date night and Katie felt heat flush again to her cheeks. Silly of her. Just because Cassie had said that about her and her husband didn't mean that Josh thought she considered this a date. He probably hadn't even noticed what Cassie had said.

"All right!" Jillian clapped for attention then launched into a cheerful explanation of candle wax temperatures, fragrance ratios, and wick sizing. The aunts were already two steps ahead, sniffing every fragrance bottle on the table.

"This one smells like a handsome cowboy." Aunt Liz rolled her eyes and one shoulder.

Elbowing her sister, Vicki sniffed at a fragrance. "Ooh, this one smells like a handsome cowboy after a shower."

"Okay, ladies," hiding a giggle of her own, Jillian gently removed a bottle from Aunt Liz's hand, "let's stay family friendly."

The two women continued to tease and banter over different fragrances, looking for something that resembled *bling*.

Katie bit back a grin and focused on stirring their melting wax. The heat from the burner warmed her face, or maybe that was just the proximity to Josh. He'd rolled up his sleeves, revealing forearms that were—well, distracting.

"Okay!" Jillian's voice rang out again. "While your wax is melting, it's time to pick your fragrance. I've got about twenty options here. You can mix and match, but I'd recommend starting simple."

Katie moved to the fragrance station, studying the labels. Vanilla. Lavender. Pine. Cinnamon.

Josh appeared beside her, close enough that their arms brushed. "What do you think?"

"I don't know." She shrugged, keeping her eyes on the fragrances. What was it about having this man close that had her forgetting her own name? "What do you like?"

"I'm not picky."

"That's not helpful." She chuckled.

Smiling at her, he picked up a bottle labeled "Fresh Linen" sniffed, winced and shaking his head, muttered, "Definitely not that."

She laughed, reaching for another option. "How about this? Cedar and sage."

He leaned in to smell it, close enough that she could feel his breath on her hand. "Yeah. That's good."

Heat once again rose to her cheeks. She was going to have to stop doing that before people started to think she had caught something like scarlet fever.

They returned to their station with the fragrance oil, and Jillian demonstrated how to test the wax temperature with a thermometer. Katie held the thermometer while Josh stirred, their heads bent close together over the pot.

"You're doing great," he murmured.

"I haven't done anything yet."

"You picked a good scent. That counts."

She glanced up at him, finding his eyes already on her. The moment stretched, and for just a second she wondered what it might be like to live in a place like Honeysuckle with street fairs, friendly neighbors, goofy aunts, and men like Josh.

Across the table, the aunts discovered Jillian's glitter.

"Oh dear Lord," Jillian gasped. "Glitter doesn't melt into wax."

"Then why do you have it?" Aunt Vicki glared at her niece.

"For decorating, not pouring." Jill tried to retrieve the glitter from the two older women, but it was a lost cause. Glitter swirled through their melted wax like a snow globe.

Rachel cackled. "I think y'all are going to be the proud parents of the first West Texas disco-ball candle."

Biting back a grin, Josh leaned into her and murmured, "I kind of want one."

Katie giggled. She kind of wanted one too. This whole little adventure was proving to be more entertaining than she'd expected. And the company was pretty nice too. She actually wished it were a real date. Then she'd have something to look forward to when the candle making was over.

Just then, the door opened, the wind chimes jingled, and Katie glanced up in time to see two women standing transfixed at the sight of glitter-covered aunts, endless laughter, men in aprons, and slap happy adults holding mason jars like they were trophies.

"Oh wow," one woman uttered. "This looks really… fun."

Jillian turned, beaming like she'd been waiting for this moment her entire life. "Would you like to join us?"

They nodded eagerly. Within minutes, two more wandered in, drawn by the noise and lights. From the way Jillian and the aunts interacted, the new attendees did not appear to be locals. Just what everyone hoped for.

The newcomers settled in, more wine was poured, and while their candles set, they worked on another scent.

Stirring the wax once again, Josh glanced up at her. "Having fun?"

Katie really loved how a lazy smile often played at his lips. "Yeah. I really am."

Still watching her more than the wax, his grin widened. "Me too."

Now all she had to figure out was what the heck was she supposed to do now?

CHAPTER NINE

Josh wasn't sure when he'd stopped listening to the clatter of tonight's dinner dishes and started watching the way Katie laughed with Jackie. By the time it was decided that Monopoly was out and cards were in, he wished that he could just sit and watch her a little longer. Okay, maybe a lot longer.

Folks moved around the massive dining room table. Preston and Sara Sue excused themselves from the evening's entertainment, as did Rachel and her husband, but the rest of the clan looked a tad too eager for Josh's liking.

"Josh," Alice pointed to a chair at the opposite end of the table, "you sit over there. Katie to your left, Carson to your right."

People continued to shuffle around the table, making themselves at home. Jillian muttered something about *thank heaven it wasn't Monopoly* before taking a seat next to Katie.

"Continental Rummy," Alice announced. "Only jokers are wild." She looked to Josh and Katie. "It's an easy game. Like Rummy, you have to make runs and multiples of a kind, we'll start with two three of a kind. Six cards are dealt. If you want to draw a card when it's not your turn, you toss a coin into the jar and pick up your card as well as a spare card for penalty. Once you have the required cards, you can go down, but you can't place any cards elsewhere until the next round."

Josh glanced around the table. Carson whistled as he organized his chips by color. Garret's expression couldn't have been more serious if he'd been preparing his tax return. Smiling at Alice, Cassie shuffled the decks. With this many people more than one deck of cards was required. With the ease of her former profession, Cassie shuffled the cards in sections before shuffling them all at once. Setting the cards to her right, Kade cut the deck and set the remainder in the center of the table.

Reaching for the first dealt card, Josh tilted his head slightly, leaning into Katie. "Ever played?"

Sitting stiffly, she seemed to nervously nibble at her bottom lip as she barely shook her head—another endearing habit he tried to ignore. "Not this version."

"Me neither. Looks like we're both in trouble."

Josh picked up his cards, immediately spotting he had absolutely nothing worth keeping. Across from him, Carson already looked pleased with his hand. Meanwhile, Garret reorganized his cards for the third time with the concentration of a bomb defusal expert.

"First round is two sets of three of a kind," Alice reminded them. "Simple enough."

Simple. Right. Josh glanced at Katie's profile as she studied her cards, bottom lip caught between her teeth again. That little habit was becoming dangerously distracting.

Garret drew from the deck and discarded. Play moved around the table. When it reached Garret again, he plucked a card from the discard pile without hesitation, rearranged something in his hand, and set down his cards with quiet confidence. "Down."

"Already?" Jillian groaned.

"Math teacher," Garret shrugged, not even trying to hide his smug smile.

Three rounds in, Josh had burned through half his chips buying cards out of turn. Katie wasn't faring much better. Every time she reached for the pile, she'd mutter something under her breath that made him want to lean closer to hear.

Who was he kidding, even if she were silent, he'd still have to fight the urge to lean in closer. "Having trouble there?"

She drew yet another penalty card. "That one," she nodded toward Garret, "is a card shark."

"You heard him, math teacher," Josh grinned. "Comes with the territory."

"And I'm down, and out." Cassie splayed her cards on the table, and leaning back, grinned like the Cheshire cat. Not a single penalty card. How had she... and then he remembered. His buddy's new wife used to be a Vegas card dealer, but more than that, the woman had a memory for cards and numbers that could make them all very rich if she'd ever sit at the other side of a Vegas card game.

"Okay," Katie shook her head, and setting down one card at a time, counted her points. "Maybe we *should* have played Monopoly." Calling out her points, she heaved a sigh and leaned back in her seat.

He couldn't tell if her teasing was in earnest or playful fun, but either way, Monopoly or cards, the only thing Josh was sure of, was that he was no longer frustrated by *why* he was here, he was just very glad *here* was with Katie. And wasn't that an interesting revelation?

Katie had played cards before. Rummy, even. But never quite like this.

The Sweet family treated Continental Rummy like a contact sport. Alice presided from her end of the table with the benevolent authority of a referee who wasn't afraid to call fouls. Cassie shuffled with the kind of casual expertise that should have been Katie's first warning. And Garret— Garret approached the game with an intensity that suggested national security depended on his next card.

Katie glanced at her cards, then glanced up, speaking to anyone at the table. "What are we doing now?"

"Two runs of four." Alice smiled at her guest.

Runs. That was like a straight, which meant four cards in a row of the same suit. Too bad she seemed to have all pairs. Two sevens, two fours, a pair of kings, a nine of spades, and a three of hearts. Where were the dumb pairs in the last round when she'd needed them?

Beside her, Josh rearranged his cards for the third or fourth, or was it fifth time? Sitting so close, with every shift, his elbow brushed against hers. At first, she'd barely noticed, but now, she had a rising urge to lean into his touch. How crazy was that?

Another round of play and Katie found herself biting down on her back teeth. Between the free draw and the discards anyone would think she should be able to piece together at least one run of four but so far, no such luck.

Josh's elbow rubbed against hers again, only this time, the pressure remained warm and solid against her as he leaned in and whispered, "You doing okay?"

Not wanting to say something stupid like, *dang you smell good*, she opted to simply nod, and just for the hell of it, rearranged her cards in no particular order.

Another round and across the table, Garret went down first. Again. Except, she was pretty sure he still held more cards in his hand than the original eight.

"Show-off," Carson muttered good-naturedly.

"It's strategy." Garret flashed a toothy grin.

Pointing her nose in her brother's direction, Jillian rolled her eyes. "I'm pretty sure the idea of going down is to have fewer cards in your hands than you were dealt." Now she shook her head. "I don't think your strategy got the memo."

Katie had to bite down hard on her lower lip to stop from laughing. First at Jillian's jabbing remark and then at Garret's crestfallen expression. These folks sure knew how to raise the drama on an ordinary card game.

"Ha, ha," Garret quipped back, carefully watching the cards played in the next two rounds. When Jillian went down, still holding a couple of cards in her hand, Garret grinned a little wider, practically bouncing in his seat when his turn came around and he placed two cards on Jillian's hand. "Read 'em and weep."

Chuckling quietly, Cassie shook her head. "Don't count your winnings yet." In two swift moves, she laid down both runs of four and without a single card left in her hands, grinned up at her brother-in-law. "I believe the expression is… read 'em and weep."

Katie had to cover her mouth with her hand to stop from laughing. Losing the game or not, she was loving every minute of the evening. Her entire life, this was what she'd been missing—the teasing, the noise, the way they all poked at each other but never with real malice. Growing up an only child had been quiet, peaceful, but lonely in too many different ways—until now.

Next round, shaking her head, Katie tossed a chip into the pot, stole a card and mumbled softly, "I feel like I'm subsidizing the family winnings."

"I know how you feel," Josh muttered back.

Determined to get the three sets of three of a kind before anyone else went down, she rearranged her cards and made a single mistake of glancing over at Josh, catching a wide smile and eyes focused on her not his cards. Her breath caught and the noise of the table faded—Alice's laughter, Garret's groan as Kade went down, Jillian's triumphant cheer. It all blurred into background static.

"And I'm out." Grinning wider than ever, Cassie set her cards down, scooped up the winning pile of chips, and leaned back.

The moment gone, Katie blinked. "How do you keep doing that?"

Kade slung his arm around his wife's shoulder. "She counts cards."

"She what?" Katie knew her mouth was hanging open.

"Vegas card dealer," Carson spoke as though that explained everything.

Shaking her head, Cassie leveled her gaze with Katie. "My former career is not relevant. I've always been really good with numbers and learned to count cards as a kid in foster care. I remember every card played and don't pick up spare cards because the math doesn't work. Not if I'm patient."

"Don't you ever pick up cards?" Katie asked meekly.

"Sure," Cassie shrugged. "If the math is there."

"Math," she chuckled softly. Who knew a degree in mathematics and statistics would be totally useless in a simple family card game.

By the last round of twelve cards, Katie couldn't believe lady luck had finally found her. Three runs of four and she had a good start to all three.

Josh's elbow nudged hers, only this time she realized it wasn't an accident. When she glanced up at him, he was smiling down on her. Leaning in a little closer, he dipped his head and the warmth of this breath on her neck had her swallowing hard. "You have a terrible poker face."

Blinking twice, she struggled to pry her tongue from the roof of her mouth before finally managing to utter, "Whatever do you mean?"

Chuckling, he didn't move. "If you don't have a winning hand, I'm a monkey's uncle."

"You shouldn't speak that way about your family," she teased, biting back a smile.

Josh burst out laughing, every set of eyes at the table turned on him and Katie felt the heat rising in her cheeks. What was this man doing to her?

CHAPTER TEN

A cold, wet nose pressed against Josh's palm, followed immediately by the jingle of metal tags. In the dead silence of the country night, the soft sound might as well have been a cymbal crash. Forcing one eye open, Josh groaned. Except for the sliver of moonlight cutting through the blinds, the room was pitch black.

Raider whined again, a low, desperate sound that vibrated against the side of the mattress.

"All right, buddy. I hear you." Josh pushed the quilt aside. He knew better than to bolt upright. That lesson had been learned the hard way over the last few weeks since the explosion—move too fast, and the world tilts on its axis like a carnival ride gone wrong. Instead, he sat up by degrees, gripping the edge of the mattress and waited for the fluid in his inner ear to settle. One. Two. Three, he counted the seconds in the dark. The dizziness was there, a low-grade hum in the background, but the room wasn't spinning. Progress. "Let's go," he whispered.

Raider needed no encouragement. The shepherd's nails clicked against the vinyl floor as he moved slowly toward the door. Josh stood, locking his knees, finding his center of gravity. Reaching for the belly band, he carefully slipped it under Raider, holding it in one hand as his free hand caressed the wall, his fingers trailing against the plaster for orientation. Leaning to one side, he opened the door, surprised to have a soft, golden glow spill from the kitchen, shining a beacon across the hallway floor.

Josh paused, his hand still on the doorframe. Raider didn't wait; the dog tugged him toward the light, his tail giving a rare, low wag. Josh followed, the two moving slowly, Josh's bare feet silent on the wood in complete contrast to the rhythmic tapping of Raider's nails on the floor.

At the sight of the refrigerator door wide open, he came to a sudden stop. It was too late for the family to be up, and too early for Alice to be making breakfast. Staring into the depths of the fridge, Katie shifted her weight from one foot to the other, her robe wrapped behind wiggling just enough to set him off balance in a way that had nothing to do with his ears. Smiling at the sight before him, he paused in the doorway. "Casing the joint?"

Katie jumped, a small jar of pickles nearly slipping from her hand. She bobbled it, caught it against her chest, and spun around. Her eyes went wide, then softened when she saw him. "Good grief." She let out a breath that made her chest heave and his balance waver once more. "I didn't hear you coming."

"Sorry. Walking softly is an occupational hazard. Though Raider here doesn't seem to have that problem." Smiling at her, he nodded toward the fridge. "Find anything good?"

"I was told there was leftover fried chicken." She turned back to the shelves, her voice dropping to a conspiratorial whisper. "But I think Alice might have hidden it. She runs a tight ship."

Raider nudged at his leg, letting out a whine that reminded Josh his current mission had nothing to do with the fridge and everything to do with the back door. "He needs out."

"Oh, of course." Katie didn't hesitate. Twisting around, she set the pickles on the counter and rushed to the back door, flipping on the porch light and grabbing a flashlight that hung on a nearby hook. "Despite the blanket of stars in the sky, it gets awfully dark out there."

He nodded, and as they walked past, Raider seemed to bump against her, not so much an accident as it seemed a gesture of thanks, perhaps a doggy version of a fist bump.

Out on the porch, Katie clicked the flashlight on, sweeping the beam across shrubs at the foot of the back steps. "Should I help getting him down the stairs?"

Josh thought for a second. The dog seemed lighter in the band tonight, to be bearing more of his own weight. "Let me take this off and see how he does on his own for a few minutes."

Gingerly, Raider made his way down the stairs and took an immediate interest in the smell of every shrub along the back of the house, marking them one at a time.

"He's moving better," she noted, her voice low.

"Yeah. Time, rest, and that elevated bed all help." He wished the same for himself, but he wasn't sure if there was enough time and rest in the world to fix him.

She crossed the porch to stand beside him, her gaze on the distant, dark horizon.

"Penny for your thoughts?" He didn't know where that came from, something his grandmother used to say when he was a little boy, but it seemed to fit the moment.

"All those stars, all that black of night, it's like the stars are hiding the night's secrets."

Well that was a different thought. "Secrets huh?"

Staring ahead, she nodded.

"Like what?"

She didn't face him, but the corner of her mouth tilted up. "Probably a little of everything. Secret lovers sneaking out at night to steal a few moments together. Children reading under the blanket with a flashlight when they should be sleeping."

"Or teenage boys stealing glimpses of their dad's *Playboy* magazine."

Now she turned to face him, one brow higher than the other. "The voice of experience?"

Slapping his hand on his chest, and widening his eyes, he feigned shock. "Me?"

To his delight, that had her laughing, before turning back to see Raider working his way slowly back to the porch steps. "I alphabetize my spice racks."

"Excuse me?"

She turned to face him. "Jackie invited me to visit so I would stop organizing my closets. I didn't have the heart to tell her I not only organized, I alphabetized my spices. And maybe my DVD collection."

"I see." He held back a grin. "So, what you're saying is the stars are keeping our secrets too?"

Tilting her head, she leveled her gaze with his. "What secrets are they keeping for you," she straightened and flashed a bright smile under the porch light, "since you didn't steal a peek at your dad's magazines."

Debating what to say next, he decided to stick with levity. "Busted zipper."

"Excuse me?"

"A busted zipper did me in. New tactical gear for special night maneuvers. Worked great. Until we returned home. The zipper was totally stuck and when I yanked at it with sheer brute force—"

"Mm hm," she cut him off. "Men are good at that."

"So I've heard. Anyhow, I proceeded to break the dumb thing and ruin any chance of getting out of it unnoticed."

"What happened?"

"My buddy had to cut me out of it, then we had to come up with a good reason to give our CO, and the rest of my team made a point not to let me forget what happened, especially after a few beers."

"You win. That definitely beats my spice rack."

Raider barked, and Josh could see he was now at their feet but a bit wobbly on his. "I'd better put this back on and get him to that restful bed for more recovery time."

"Need help?"

"No. We've got this." He slid the band around him, took two steps, then stopped. Nothing about going back to his quiet room appealed right now. Spending more time with Katie, on the other hand… "Did you say fried chicken?

Katie followed Josh and Raider inside, letting the screen latch with a soft click. "Fried chicken," she headed for the fridge, "the breakfast of champions. Or insomniacs."

His movements slow and deliberate, Josh crossed the room, unhooked the belly band from beneath Raider, and stretching his hand forward, let Raider sniff him a moment, and when the dog licked his hand, he shifted to scratching behind his ear.

"He's taken a real shine to you." At first it had surprised her how the dog had warmed up to Josh and not Kade the trained handler, but from what she could see, it seemed pretty obvious the feeling was mutual.

"I think he's just hoping for some of that fried chicken."

"Fried chicken. Right." She spun around and pulled the fridge door open. "I think I saw the container on the bottom shelf earlier." She leaned in, moving several items out of the way. "Behind the yogurt. Alice buys yogurt in tubs the size of small swimming pools."

"Good hiding spot." Josh leaned against the butcher-block island, his stance wide, his hands behind him. Whether that was military habit, or an attempt to keep his balance, she wasn't sure.

Spotting the tell-tale Tupperware tucked behind a gallon of Greek yogurt and a formidable tub of potato salad, she grabbed the container and tucking the tub against her with one arm, she spun around and held the other container up like the Stanley Cup. "Found it."

Bumping the door shut with her hip, she set the prize on the island and peeled back the lid. The scent of savory spices wafted up, instantly making her mouth water.

"I'll get the plates." Carefully turning around to reach the upper cabinets, Josh pulled two down and then, one hand on the counter, slowly turned back around.

Setting the food down, she kept her gaze on him. Definitely keeping his balance, she decided, wishing there was something she could do to help him heal up faster.

Taking a seat beside her at the table, Josh reached in and snagged a drumstick. "The colonel has nothing on Alice. Best fried chicken this side of the Mason Dixon line—even cold."

Katie went for a thigh, then plopped a hefty scoop of potato salad beside it. For the first several bites, neither said a word, both enjoying the cold meal.

Raider collapsed with a heavy, dramatic sigh right at Josh's feet. He rested his chin on Josh's foot, his dark eyes fixed upward with laser-like intensity, tracking the movement of the chicken from the container to Josh's mouth.

"Don't even think about it." Josh shook his head at the dog.

Raider whined, a high-pitched, pathetic sound that didn't match his size or his history as a hardened military asset. He nudged Josh's shin with his wet nose.

"He's playing you." Katie wiped a crumb from the corner of her mouth. "Look at those eyebrows. He's tragic."

"I see 'em. He's a manipulator. Learned it in basic training." Josh tore off a piece of meat, ignoring the dog. "Fried chicken isn't good for dogs, but I'm glad to see his appetite improving."

"Would it be all right to give him something of his own? An apple maybe?"

"Perfect." He smiled. "Nutrients and crunch factor."

She moved to the fruit basket, grabbing a shiny green apple and the paring knife from the block. The slide of the blade through the crisp fruit sounded impossibly loud in the quiet room. She cut two thick wedges and walked back to the island.

"Compromise?" She squatted down and held out a slice.

The dog didn't lift his head, and yet his eyes followed her every move. She could see him debating if he wanted the apple enough to trust her. When he took another few seconds, Josh took a slice, set it on his open palm and held it out to the dog.

Immediately Raider snatched up the piece.

Josh gave him a couple more before turning to Katie. "You try this time."

She had remained low to the ground at Josh and Raider's side, but wasn't so sure the poor baby was going to want the apple from her anymore than before, but she did what Josh had done and set the slice on her palm, holding it out, giving the dog time to make up his mind. Unlike before, this time Raider took a single glance up at her before taking the apple slice. "He took it!"

"Don't sound so surprised. Dog has good taste."

Now she was sure her cheeks had to be burning red. "Thank you," was all she managed to say before shoving a slice of apple into her own mouth and retaking her seat.

An arms length away, he reached out, his hand hovering for a split second before his thumb brushed the corner of her mouth.

Katie stopped breathing. Despite the heat in her cheeks, she froze, her heart hammering a frantic rhythm against her ribs.

"Crumb," he whispered.

The distinct groan of a floorboard settling directly above their heads drew their gazes heavenward.

"Alice," he mouthed.

"Should we..." Katie pointed vaguely toward the dishwasher.

"Hide the evidence?" Josh chuckled. "I'm sure she won't mind, but..."

Unable to stop smiling, she nodded. "I'll put the dishes in the dishwasher."

Josh pushed to his feet. "I'll put the containers away."

They moved together, a silent, synchronized cleanup crew. Josh shoved the chicken back into the fridge, burying it the way they'd found it behind the tub of potato salad. She wiped the table down, erasing the crumbs and the grease rings. It was domestic. It was simple. And it was terrifyingly comfortable.

CHAPTER ELEVEN

"**F**ind her!"

Kade's command cracked through the crisp morning air, sharp and authoritative, a stark contrast to the lazy atmosphere that usually hung over the ranch when no one was working.

Leaning against the rough cedar post of the corral fence, Josh crossed his arms and watched the master at work. Or rather, the masters. Brady, the Sweet family's retired Military Working Dog, didn't look retired today. The moment the command registered, the German Shepherd's posture shifted. Josh watched the dog's tail—low, focused, not the happy wag of playtime but the serious wag of a working animal. Brady lowered his nose, taking in a deep draft of air, filtering through the scents of horse manure, gasoline, and dry dust to find the one specific track he'd been tasked to locate.

"He's still got it," Josh murmured to himself. If Brady could still do what he was trained for after all he'd been through, including retirement, maybe there was still hope for Josh. A week ago, standing this long without holding onto the fence would have sent the horizon tilting sideways. Today, the world remained mostly upright, though he kept his shoulder against the post, just in case. His attention remained mostly on the dog working a zigzag pattern across the open yard, ignoring the distractions of hands working in the barn and the distant lowing of cattle. It was impressive.

The exercises had Josh's mind drifting back to rehab at the hospital. Stepping off to the side, out of earshot from the folks on the porch, he dialed the hospital.

The phone in Boglioli's room rang twice. "Hello."

"Hey, man. How's it going?" Josh tried to infuse his voice with positive energy.

Aiden sighed. "Besides feeling like a flipped turtle? Could be worse."

Josh could almost see the guy shrugging on the other end of the line. "Flipped turtle?"

"You should see some of these floor exercises. It's crazy. And the names! I mean, who thought *dead bugs* was a good name for a recovery exercise?"

He shouldn't have laughed, but he couldn't help it. "Dead bug? I'm going to agree with you on that one. The important thing is to be making progress."

"That I am, Sarge. Off the crutches. I'm supposed to be set free soon." His voice seemed to lift a bit.

"Good. Very good to hear. Where to next?"

"My case worker hasn't told me yet. Honestly, I'm not sure she knows. How about you? How's the ranch treating you? Got your balance back yet?"

"Getting there." He was almost afraid to say he felt better for fear the universe would jinx him and throw something new at him. "A man can get used to the way they take care of you here."

"Really?"

He could certainly get used to one particular person here at the ranch, but that wasn't what Boglioli was asking. "Even Colonel Sanders can't beat Mrs. Sweet's fried chicken."

"Oh man, don't mention food. I swear whoever the chef is here, the guy graduated from the Garbage Collectors Culinary School."

For the next few minutes they chatted about the other soldiers caught in the blast, about the hot Texas weather, and how there wasn't a single place in the state to get a decent marinara sauce.

"Got to go. Atila the Hun is here for my next workout."

Something in his tone told Josh this Atila was of a feminine nature. "Blonde or Brunette?"

"Redhead." A smile came through in his voice. "See you later, Sarge."

And with that, Josh grinned and returned his attention to the training session across the way. Brady was one heck of a dog.

Satisfied with the scent cone, Brady accelerated, heading straight for a large mound of loose hay and empty feed sacks stacked near the equipment shed. He circled it once, let out a sharp, confirming bark, and his stance stiff and royal like a pedigree dog on point.

"Good boy!" Kade beamed at his former K9 partner, hurrying to catch up to where the dog alerted.

A pile of burlap sacks shifted, dry leaves fluttered, and like a jack in the box, Cassie burst from her hiding spot, laughing at Brady's enthusiastic tongue bath and playfully scratching the scruff of his neck. "Okay, okay! You found me! You're the smartest boy in the whole world."

Josh wasn't sure if it was Brady or Cassie that had Kade beaming down at his wife and dog. Absurd. Of course he knew Kade loved his dog, but he adored his wife. Heaving a deep sigh, Josh's gaze drifted naturally, inevitably, toward the ranch house porch and the two women enjoying the show.

Sitting in one of the dark green rockers with a bowl of garden fresh green beans in her lap, Kade's mother smiled softly at her son and Brady. But the one who had him looking over his shoulder was Katie, sitting on the top step, her eyes twinkling, her smile, wide, and her cheers for the work dog worthy of a pro sports team.

When their gazes briefly collided, the unexpected expanse of that already wide grin made his heart do a little somersault. Had just a smile ever had him on high alert? Made him want to smile and not stop?

"Earth to Josh."

He blinked, turning back to find Kade standing three feet away, Brady seated proudly at Kade's heel, looking pleased with his morning's work. "Good boy, Brady." Ignoring the cheeky grin on his buddy's face, Josh leaned over and scratched behind the German Shepherd's ear.

"Doesn't matter how gray the muzzle gets, the drive is still there." Kade reached down to gently pet the top of his former partner's head.

"He did good."

"He did." Kade sighed, the humor fading into a look of reluctance. He glanced at his watch.

"Time to go?" he asked.

"Almost."

The reality of the moment settled between them. Kade was going back to the unit, back to the work they both loved. Josh was staying here, fighting a war against gravity and inner ear fluid.

As if his longtime friend had read his mind, Kade lifted his chin at his buddy. "You're looking better, man. Only a week and you're standing straighter. Less… green around the gills."

Only a week. Seven days. Seven days of small victories. Raider eating more and walking without the belly strap. His own balance improving in increments so slight he almost didn't notice until he did. "I'm getting there. Slowly." Too slowly for his liking. He still needed to move carefully, avoid nodding or shaking his head, and fast turns remained out of the question.

Almost vibrating with restrained energy, Brady nudged Kade's leg.

"Okay, boy." Kade laughed.

Cassie came up on Kade's side and his arm immediately looped around her waist. "You up for another run?" Kade posed the question to his wife, but Brady was the one dancing around his former handler as if he'd won the doggie lottery.

"All right, boy." Cassie squatted down and with a hand on each side of the dog's head, rubbed his neck and kissed the top of his head. "Close your eyes and count to ten."

Chuckling softly, Kade shook his head and rolled his eyes, eyes that brimmed with love for his wife. Even Josh found her silly joke amusing and had to bite back a laugh.

Kade handed Josh the leash. "One more time. Keep him looking away a few minutes."

Turning away from him and the dog, Cassie lightly leaned into him. Together they walked away toward the barn. How well they fit, the synchronization of their steps despite the difference in their heights, the sparkle in both their eyes as if they were the only two people in the state of Texas, reminded Josh of what a lifetime partnership should look like. He couldn't help it, the thought had him looking toward the porch. The scene of total domesticity, a throwback to the days of Norman Rockwell and the American Gothic portrait, sent an odd sense of longing rushing through his veins.

His gaze shifted to where Kade and Cassie had disappeared around the barn then back to Katie chatting easily with Alice. Some things a soldier like him had no business considering—Katie deserved more than what he had to offer.

Snap. The crisp sound of another green bean meeting its fate in Alice's bowl punctuated the simple ways of life on a Texas ranch. Katie honestly didn't think anyone snapped the ends off green beans any more. Shielding her eyes from the sun to get a better look at the man by the fence, Katie couldn't help but smile.

The whole training exercise had been fascinating to watch. Now, Josh was doing an admirable job of holding back a hundred pounds of eager German Shepherd. The dog's gaze was fixed on a distant point, his muscles were sharp and tight, and even though she'd never trained a service dog, she knew Brady was just waiting for his next command. She remembered Kade mentioning in passing one day that service dogs needed structure and a job to avoid poor behavior. Not that Brady ever displayed poor behavior, but he clearly loved having a job to do.

"That dog is amazing." Alice tossed another bean into the bowl.

From this distance, she couldn't hear what Josh was saying to the dog, but she could see his ears flick and then his rear end settle into the dirt. That dog had patience to spare.

Kade came walking back to where Josh and Brady waited and gave the dog a wad of red cloth to sniff as Josh handed the leash back to him.

"I wonder where Cassie's hiding this time." Katie tried to see what the cloth was, but they were standing too far away. So far Cassie had hidden behind the barn, under the leaves, and earlier she'd actually been laying flat on the tool shed roof. Though how the heck she'd gotten up there without anyone noticing Katie didn't have a clue.

The dog stopped sniffing and pulled hard against his leash.

Unclipping the restraint, Kade pointed ahead. "Search!"

She'd noticed that he didn't always use the same word. Later, she'd have to ask him why he didn't simply say 'find her' as he had before.

Brady launched himself forward, a black-and-tan blur streaking toward the barn. Josh stayed put, arms crossing over his chest, a small, satisfied smile touching his lips as the dog went to work.

A couple of times Brady stopped, his head lifted momentarily to the air before returning his nose to the ground. Each time she wondered what the animal was up to, and each time, he moved further down the field.

Curiosity getting the better of her, she stood and walked to where Josh remained by the corral.

"Hey there." He smiled at her. Why was it the simple timbre of his voice always made her cheeks flush with heat? It didn't matter if he was saying something pleasant or reading a technical manual, the man's voice was like deep, dark, warm honey and she couldn't get enough of it.

With Kade following close behind him, Brady turned toward the east until he and his handler were out of sight.

"Cassie must have gone pretty far this time?" She didn't dare look at Josh for fear that her face would color like a roasted sugar beet.

"Maybe."

His tone was so non-committal and yet all knowing that she turned to read his face. At that moment, a single sharp bark came from Brady along with an eruption of cheers and praise.

"Come on." Josh put his hand on the small of her back and urged her forward.

Just what she needed, hot cheeks, a warm back, and every chance of self-combusting.

Only halfway to where Brady and Kade had disappeared from view, Kade, Cassie, and Benny came into the clearing.

"He found Benny."

"Yep." Josh slowed his steps, letting the others catch up to them.

"I knew he was a good work dog." Removing his hat, Benny wiped his forehead with the red bandana that Brady had sniffed to find him. "But I had no idea he was this good. I was surrounded by enough fertilizer and manure to throw off the best bloodhound."

His chest puffed and his smile wide, Kade patted the dog's head. "Brady's better than a blood hound." At that, Kade flipped his wrist and checked his watch. "Playtime is over. I've got to hit the road if I want to be back on base before someone reports me AWOL."

Josh carefully moved to one side, falling into step beside Kade and the others. "Give the guys my best."

"I will." Kade looped his arm around his wife again while Brady ran ahead to the house and Benny veered off to return to his work in the barn.

At the porch, Alice set the green beans to one side and pushed to her feet. "Will you be back soon?"

Pulling away from his wife, Kade wrapped his arms around his mom. "As soon as the brass gives me a little time off."

Nodding her head into his shoulder, Alice's smile was a little stiff, but she bobbed her chin once again and stepped back. "Well," she sighed, "at least I know you won't get blown up by insurgents in some sandy country on the other side of the world."

"It won't be long." Kade reassured his mother.

The way Josh tensed beside her, she got the impression his mind had just gone back to a convoy in Texas that had blown up sending several good men to the hospital. No point in anyone mentioning that to Alice.

A few more hugs, a long kiss for his wife that had everyone developing a sudden interest in the ceiling, and Kade swung his duffel over his shoulder and waved once more from halfway to his rental vehicle.

Josh nudged her with his arm and tipped his head toward the house.

Nodding, she followed him inside allowing Alice and Cassie a little privacy as the man they both loved rode off the property.

"I know he's supposed to be a working dog, but to me it looked like he was just having fun."

"That's because he was. Like people, if you love what you do, you'll never work a day in your life."

"My mom always said that. I love my job, but it still feels like work."

"But you like it?"

"Most of the time."

"You're on furlough from the shutdown?"

"That's right. I'm under contract to the DOD. Lots of perks. I get a bazillion weeks of vacation and every other Friday off. When necessary I can work from home, so it has a lot of positives."

"Any word on when you'll be called back?"

She shrugged. "Who knows. The news thought it would be over as soon as I got here and yet…"

"Here we still are." He made a sound not quite a scoff, not quite a chuckle. "Who'd have thunk. Two people who both work in one way or another for Uncle Sam, and for one reason or other are forced to take time off from a job we like."

Since being here, meeting him, she had to admit, she wasn't so sure she liked her job near as much as she'd thought. Odds were, he was probably considering his own future. "Are you looking forward to going back?"

He heaved a slow heavy sigh. "Right now, I'm not very sure of anything. I feel like I'm in a dream and any day now I'll be forced back into the real world."

"They're pretty lucky."

Josh's head tipped slightly, his brows buckled in confusion.

"The Sweets. All of them. There doesn't seem to be a dysfunctional bone in anyone's body and the whole darn town seems like it fell out of a Norman Rockwell painting."

Now he chuckled in earnest. "I know what you mean." A soft gentle smile came to rest on his lips.

That blasted smile had her feeling warm all over and wishing they could walk the rest of the way arm in arm like Kade and Cassie. Almost shaking her head at her own thoughts, she silently scolded herself. This man would eventually recover and return to the military that would deploy him who knew where—including, as Alice had put it, to some sandy country across the world—that was his reality. All the while she'd be back in Houston. Nothing good could come from getting close and cozy with this man. Except she didn't like that one bit. Not one little bit. Suddenly, she very much wanted to get closer, if not cozy, and that, like it or not, was not her best idea ever. Or was it?

CHAPTER TWELVE

"**A**tta boy."

Over the last several days, Raider seemed to be improving exponentially. The stitches had healed, his gait was slow but steady, and his disposition was now demanding something to do. Something more than lie around the house accepting scratches and treats. So far the only person Raider had cottoned to unconditionally was Josh, and Katie was his next favorite. Josh had not figured out what the dog had against the rest of the family. He wasn't mean to them, just hesitant and as a result, distant. He still slept mostly on the raised dog bed, but sometimes, especially during meals at the kitchen table, the dog would rest at Josh's feet. Like now.

"Funny how even off duty, he still positions himself like a war dog." Alice Sweet poured a cup of tea for herself and held the kettle up. "Want more?"

"Thank you." Josh had been working at the table, nothing critical, keeping up with emails and other communications with Kade and his team, checking on the injured and the recently recovered, but mostly, he'd been researching, for the umpteenth time, options and prognosis for his condition. Closing his laptop, he held out his empty mug.

"Ooh, looks like I got here just in the nick of time." Katie practically bounced into the room. Her long blonde hair pulled back in a sloppy ponytail swished back and forth against her back. She looked better than great.

"The news still reports that Congress is digging their heels in and butting heads. Are you hearing anything different?"

She shook her head and that same easy flowing ponytail swayed, taunting him to run his fingers through the silken strands.

He came within seconds of forgetting the tea and sitting on his hands before he did something really stupid.

"Nothing." Katie flopped into the chair across the table from him. "For once, the media seems to know exactly what they're talking about."

Taking a seat at the head of the table, Alice cupped her warm mug and laughed. "I really do miss Walter Cronkite."

"Walter Cronkite?" Katie frowned. "The news anchor from the sixties?"

"Yeah, well. I'm not that old." Alice chuckled softly. "He was on the air until the 80s, and then the mantra for news desks became, *If it bleeds, it leads.* Such a shame."

Katie shrugged. "If I were still in Houston I'd probably be going stir crazy by now. Heck, I was practically stir crazy two weeks ago!"

"And we are delighted to have you wait this out with us." Alice blew over the brim of her cup. "Have we heard from Jackie today?"

"As a matter of fact," Katie smiled, "I'm going into town to meet her for lunch. The kids have a half day today, then the teachers have some kind of meeting before they have to prep for the parent teacher meetings tonight. Jackie has to be at the school for the meetings, but since she's only a class aide, she gets to skip the meeting and have a long lunch with me."

"Perfect." Alice reached for a butter cookie on the plate in the middle of the table that had been calling Josh's name since he sat down. If he didn't get out of here soon he was going to cave and eat the whole platter of cookies. With his lack of exercise since the explosion, he needed all that sugar and carbs like he needed the proverbial hole in the head. What he really needed was to move. To get out of the kitchen. "I have to pick up a prescription at the pharmacy. I'd be happy to give you a ride. Save gas on two trips."

To his relief, her face lit up at the suggestion like a little kid taking in the toy store window. "That would be great."

At his feet, Raider's head tipped, his ears twitched, and he glanced from him to Katie. More and more he believed that animal understood every word anyone said in English. He almost laughed to himself; he wouldn't be surprised if this smart animal understood more than English. "You itching to go for a ride too?"

Raider's head straightened and his tail swiped left and right on the cold floor.

"Is that a good idea?" Katie's gaze narrowed, not from confusion or irritation, but concern.

As if not trusting what Josh would say, Raider pushed up into a sitting position and Josh would have sworn the darn dog nodded yes to her.

Since Katie bit back a smile, she must have thought the same thing.

Alice shrugged. "He's had plenty of rest, maybe it's time for a little recreation."

"Then I guess I'm taking Raider to town."

Now the dog was up on all fours, his tail wagging happily from side to side and Josh didn't have the heart to tell him not yet. Instead he looked to Katie. "Is it okay if we go a little early? We could hang out at the park or something to kill time."

She shrugged. "Works for me."

It didn't take long for Katie to transfer her tea to a travel mug and grab her purse, while Josh located and hooked the leash onto Raider's collar. Everyone, including the dog, was all smiles.

Another few minutes and they were strapped in and on the road to town.

"It's getting to you, isn't it?" Leaning against the passenger door, Katie tugged at her shoulder strap and smiled at him.

"That obvious?" He kept his eyes on the road.

"That you're as restless as Raider here?" She nodded. "Yeah. I recognize that look. Same one I had after I'd rearranged my closets and cabinets and cleaned out my drawers."

"Alphabetically," he added with a smile, hoping he

hadn't said the wrong thing and delighted when she let out a sweet laugh.

"And alphabetically," she chuckled softly.

"Were you always that meticulous?"

"Thank you for that. My mother called me neurotic. For a while she worried that all my dolls were lined up on the shelf from shortest to tallest and that when I was old enough to put my own clothes away, all the clothes in my drawers, and closets, were color coded."

"Impressive." He nodded. "You would have done well in the military."

"Doubtful. I'm also allergic to rising before the sun."

"Yeah," he chuckled softly, "that would pose a problem."

"Not one you have?"

He shrugged. "As a teen I could sleep all day with the best of them, but no, I don't mind rising with the sun. Or before it." Waking early was as common in the Army and Marines as it would be to find a bear in the woods. He just hoped he could go back to the work he loved. His gaze drifted to Katie still smiling at him. Then again maybe it was time for a change…

As soon as they rolled into town, Katie noticed something a little odd. The few times she'd come down Main Street there were always people milling about. Honeysuckle, after all, was a tourist destination. Today, however, was different. There seemed to be more people and all of them ambling about, were staring at the ground. "That's odd. Don't you think?"

Josh must have not only noticed, but agreed with her. His gaze darted from one person to the other, all moving slowly like the march of the wooden soldiers, and all watching the ground. "Something is definitely up… or down," he teased. "Let me drop off the prescription and then we'll see if we can figure out what's so fascinating about the sidewalk."

"Works for me." She kept her attention on the people along the street. If she didn't know better, she'd say she was swept into an episode of the old *Twilight Zone* television show.

Plenty of room for parking in front of the drugstore, Josh hurried around the hood of the ranch truck and had taken hold of her door before she could climb out on her own. She had to admit, there was a lot to be said for the chivalrous nature of the men around here. Whether it was because they were ranchers, or in a small town, she had no idea, but either way she wasn't going to complain. Especially since helping her out of the truck meant an excuse to hold Josh's hand, even for a little while.

As soon as she was on the curb, Josh opened the back door of the old quad cab and latched Raider's leash onto his collar again. Wrapping his arms carefully around the large dog, he helped ease him out of the vehicle and onto the curb. It was sweet how he realized the dog would need help; a lot of men would have made the poor animal jump on that weak leg. She also found herself wishing that she was the dog, Josh's strong arms carrying her out of the truck. How foolish was that? All these silly hopes and dreams, anyone would think she was a teenager again.

The walk inside took a little longer as Raider needed to register and file away every new scent, and clearly there were quite a few in the several feet between the car and the pharmacy door. She loved how patient Josh was with the dog and smiled at the bond the two had built. As soon as the door opened, Katie realized something was off.

Apparently, so did Raider. The dog stiffened, his nose to the air and his tail stopped swishing. Immediately, he tugged at Josh, pulling him to the right. Josh's gaze shot to Katie as a low wailing sound came from the direction Raider was moving.

Around the corner of the last aisle, the problem became clear. Huddled on the ground a little boy, maybe six or seven years old, had his hands on his ears and was rocking forward and back, making a low whaling sound. Standing over him, a woman hovered, bargaining with the child. "Luke, how about a new unicorn lovie, you like unicorns."

Beside her, the clerk stood with a small square blanket about the size of a one foot square floor tile with a small stuffed animal head in the center. Probably the unicorn the mother spoke of.

Between the wails, and the mother's coaxing, the child repeated in a sharp shrill voice, "Not mine, not mine, don't want unicorn."

Katie didn't have to be an expert in child psychology to realize this wasn't an ordinary temper tantrum. The look of pain on the clerk's face and something akin to desperation on the mother, told Katie this was definitely way more than one spoiled child.

"We shouldn't intrude," Josh whispered, trying to tug Raider in the opposite direction.

The dog was having nothing of it. He pulled, and tugged, and began wiggling about until he had Josh so twisted up that he'd had no choice but to let go of the leash. Before Josh could grab hold and untangle it, the dog had bolted forward, knocking Josh off his feet in the process.

"Josh!" Katie dropped to his side. "Are you okay?"

Heaving a deep sigh, Josh closed his eyes for a second before meeting her gaze. "Only thing hurt is my pride. At least this time I can blame the hundred pound K9." His eyes widened and his head whipped to the right. "Raider!"

Standing up, Katie extended her hands, prepared to help him with his balance, but Josh had righted himself and didn't seem to be even a little off. His attention was so focused on the dog, she didn't think he'd thought to be careful. A small smile tugged at the corners of her lips. He was getting better.

"Raider." The sound of Josh's voice was low, but firm, and laced with a hint of concern.

As soon as Katie came out from behind him, she saw why he was concerned. The dog was lying across the little boy's back. Not moving, not speaking, just lying on him. The sheer horror on Josh's face was in complete contrast to the relieved sigh the mother had let out.

Completely confused, Katie looked to the little boy trapped under the dog. The kid was no longer rocking or making any noise. At her side, Josh stiffened. He looked as confused as she felt.

The mom extended her hand, palm out, and slowly moved closer to them. "I can't thank you enough."

Josh's brows shot up high on his forehead, but he didn't say a word.

"He lost his favorite lovie. The baseball bear one. We have three just in case of a situation like this, but today of all days, I only grabbed one. I have no idea where he dropped it, but he's been inconsolable since he noticed it missing."

"And the dog is helping?" Katie almost whispered. It was a stupid question, because the kid had shifted so the dog was still lying on him, but the little boy could wrap an arm around the dog.

"It's the pressure. Do you have autistic children? Is that why the dog knew what to do?"

Autism Spectrum. Now things were making a little sense to her.

Josh shook his head. "He's a military service dog. Injured in an explosion."

"Oh my." The woman's head whipped around and she spoke softly, "Luke, be careful with the doggy, he has an ouchie."

The child muttered, "ouchie" and shifted to a fully seated position and gently stroked the dog's fur. "It's okay, doggy. I take care of you."

Staring wistfully at her son, the mom sighed again and turned to Josh and Katie. "Are you in a hurry? I'd rather not try to separate them just yet. I think the whole town is walking from the park to here trying to find his lovie. If someone would just find it sooner than later he'll be all right." She paused, noticing Luke was smiling. "Then again, maybe we don't need it any more."

"No hurry," Josh reassured the stressed woman. "I'm just going to see about my prescription." Keeping his gaze on Raider and the little boy, Josh continued down the aisle to the pharmacist's window.

At least now they knew why so many people were wandering about watching the pavement. Small towns really were something else.

Another step and without a word, Josh grabbed hold of her hand, slowing his steps to match hers, and her heart nearly stuttered. She could feel the tension in his stance in complete contrast to the warmth of his hand. Reality was way better than any hope or dream. Her gaze rose to his profile. Strong jaw, currently clamping down on his back teeth. He was troubled, she knew that. She also knew he was kind, and considerate, and thoughtful, and holy pharmacies, she was falling for him—hard.

CHAPTER THIRTEEN

The overhead bell of the café jingled when Josh guided Raider, followed by Katie, inside. After the recent experience at the pharmacy, he expected the dog to be exhausted. Instead the animal seemed to be energized by having finally done something besides just lie around. Raider's ears were up, his nose twitching at the mouthwatering scents—or perhaps searching for another job.

"Well, well." Agnes appeared from behind the kitchen partition, wiping her hands on her apron, her eyes going straight to Raider. "I could kiss you, sweet boy."

Josh's eyebrows shot up.

"Don't look so surprised. He's our new local hero." Agnes leaned over and scratched behind the dog's ear. "I bet we can find something special for you in the kitchen."

"How did you—"

Shaking her head and making a small tsking sound, Agnes cut him off. "Mildred McEntire." At his and Katie's blank stare, she straightened and smiled. "Sorry. Mildred is our modern version of town crier. She was at the pharmacy filling a prescription when poor Luke had his meltdown. He's a sweet boy, but when he loses it, he really loses it. Everyone was doing their best to help, but this guy was the only one who could make a difference."

Beside him, Katie shifted her purse strap higher on her shoulder, looking both amused and slightly overwhelmed by small-town communication speeds.

"Katie!" Jackie's voice rang out from a booth near the back. She waved both arms. "Over here!" Her husband Garret sat beside her, already setting his menu aside, his teacher-calm expression firmly in place.

Waving back at her friend, Katie led the way to the table, having to stop at every other table as one patron or another felt the need to praise Raider. To Josh's surprise, the dog that had been so hesitant and withdrawn when they first met, didn't seem at all distressed or leery of all the humans fussing over him. As a matter of fact, Josh was willing to bet the dog was enjoying every minute of his lovefest. Talk about a full recovery.

At the booth, Josh hesitated beside Katie, his gaze darting to the empty bench seat and then over to where Jackie and Garret sat smiling up at them. For a second he considered bailing, claiming Raider was too worn out. That would be safer than sitting this close to Katie. Before he could do or say anything, Katie slid into the booth first. Sucking in a slow breath, he slid in beside her. At his feet, Raider settled in with a heavy sigh. Right about now, Josh understood exactly how the dog felt.

"Look at you." Jackie beamed down at the dog. "Already a town hero and you've only been here, what, two weeks?"

"Something like that." Josh's hand dropped automatically to scratch behind Raider's ear.

Garret nodded toward the dog. "Kade mentioned Raider was injured in an explosion. Looks like he's healing up pretty well."

"Better than I'd expect." An odd sense of pride in the dog's progress blooming inside him.

"You seem to be doing better too." Jackie reached over and took hold of her husband's hand.

"Mm." Josh nodded. The last thing he wanted was to get into the uncertainty still rumbling around in the back of his mind. Yes, his balance felt better. Yes, he was able to nod his head, though shaking still made him feel a little off kilter, but right now he was more than a little confused about what his future held. What did he want it to hold?

"Much better." A wide smile on her face, Katie looked at him and he had an overwhelming urge to grin back—so he did.

For just a moment, their gazes locked, lingered, and Josh found himself forgetting all about his vertigo, the dog, the kid with the meltdown, his career, his doubts, and had to stop himself from taking hold of her hand much the way her friends across the table had their fingers laced together.

At his feet, Raider's tail began to sweep the floor. Josh glanced down at the dog eyeing the kitchen door like he knew good things came from that direction.

Sure enough, another few seconds and Agnes appeared through those doors and came straight to their table. "Hope this is okay." She held up a large soup bone.

Raider sat up, his muscles shaking with interest, but his training and control showing through as his gaze darted from the bone to Josh, silently waiting for the next signal.

Not waiting, Agnes stepped closer to the dog and table and nudging Josh's shoulder, urged him over so she could sit at the edge of the booth. Bending over, she cradled the dog's head with one hand before feeding him the bone with the other.

His tail slowed and his eyes met Josh's. No matter how inviting, the dog was not going to take the bone until Josh gave the orders.

Katie leaned into him, her voice low, her breath warm against his neck. "Looks like you're his person now."

If he could think straight with her so close to him, he might have argued, or agreed. As it was, all he could manage was a nod at the dog with a slight gesture to take the proffered bone.

"That is one well trained dog. Good boy." Smiling, Agnes patted the top of the dog's head and pushed to her feet. "I'll be back to take your orders in a minute."

It took everything in Josh not to call for Agnes to come back and sit down so he could remain close to Katie just a little bit longer. Instead, he wondered how much trouble might he be in if he opted to simply stay pressed against Katie instead of shifting back to his original place on the bench.

With a silent sigh and a world of regret, he shifted, picked up his menu, and decided hiding from his life and

Katie was futile. Good or bad, like it or not—and he most definitely was absolutely liking it—he was also most definitely falling for Katie Lawford. And like it or not, he needed to do something about it. But what?

By the time they pulled through the Sweet Ranch gate, Raider was asleep in the back seat, bone still clutched proudly between his paws like a trophy. The animal had certainly earned his nap. Another few minutes and Raider actually led the way into the house, straight to the guest wing and his food and water.

"Here's your hat, what's your hurry," Alice teased as the dog strolled past her. "Maybe I won't give him the pupcake I baked."

"Pupcake?" From the way Josh's whole face crumpled, he most likely had no idea what the woman was talking about.

Anyone else that expression would have made him look downright foolish, but all Katie could do was smile. On him it was rather…endearing.

"I heard what he did today for young Luke," Alice continued, "so I baked him a doggie approved cake."

"Ah," Josh nodded, "pupcake."

"That's it." Alice grinned.

"News travels fast around here, doesn't it?" Katie had heard more than one story about the Honeysuckle grapevine, but this was her first experience in a front row seat.

Cassie shook her head, biting back a laugh. "Oh, you have no idea."

"From what I hear," Alice filled a tea kettle, "Mildred says the dog was downright heroic. No one else knew what to do with Luke, no one could find his lost lovie, but Raider stepped right in and calmed the boy down."

"Pressure therapy," Josh mentioned softly.

"What?" Alice asked.

"Oh, sorry. What the dog did is called pressure therapy. It's not uncommon for autistic children."

At the sound of toenails tapping, Katie's gaze turned to Raider coming into the kitchen and plopping down at Josh's feet. "Do they train military dogs to do pressure therapy?"

"Not that I know of." Josh shook his head. "But German Shepherds are exceptionally smart dogs. Maybe for him it was just instinct."

"Like the way they always position themselves between their people and the door," Alice added. "Best way to protect the family."

Josh nodded. "Something like that."

"Guess he's almost ready to go back to work." Cassie took a seat at the table.

"Not in the military." Josh reached down to scratch the dog's ears, smiling sweetly.

Katie wondered if he realized how far over he was leaning and showing no signs of dizziness before dragging her thoughts back to what he'd just said. "Why not?"

"Even though he's recovering," Josh straightened in his seat—still no sign of dizziness, "an injury like his means medical discharge from the army. He can't be deployed again and restricted duty is hard to find for a K9."

"I see." Her lips pressed into a thin line, her eyes shifting between him and the dog, she merely nodded, considering not for the first time how alike the dog and man were. For Raider it was a given he would be retired from the military, for Josh, well, that question was still up in the air. Or was it? Maybe he already knew his destiny.

"Then maybe he could be a therapy dog?" Alice stared at the dog in deep concentration.

Josh nodded. "That's what I've been considering ever since the incident was over and the little boy hugged the stuffing out of the dog. I've worked with a lot of handlers and K9s. While I'm no Kade, if I've learned anything all these years, it's to recognize a good dog when I see one, and Raider is most definitely a good dog."

"Maybe we could do some training tests," Katie turned to Josh, "the way you and Kade did with Brady, to see if

Raider would be a good candidate?"

Before Josh could respond that he'd need help from Kade, the overhead light flickered once, capturing everyone's attention, and then again before sparking and leaving them in total darkness.

"Oh my." Katie's hand reached over and clutched at Josh's arm.

For a heartbeat, no one moved. Then Alice's voice cut through the sudden darkness. "Well. That's not ideal."

Katie blinked, waiting for her eyes to adjust. Moonlight filtered through the kitchen window, casting everything in shades of gray.

"Generator should kick in any second," Alice said.

They waited. Sure enough, a distant hum started up, and the refrigerator shuddered back to life. But the overhead lights stayed dark.

"Fridge is on the generator," Alice explained, already moving toward the pantry. "Lights aren't. Give me a second."

Katie heard rustling, then the soft glow of a flashlight beam swept across the floor.

"Here we go." Alice emerged with two gas lamps and a handful of candles. "Josh, can you light these? Matches are in the drawer by the stove."

He stood carefully, feeling his way along the counter.

Katie rose to help, their hands brushing as they both reached for the matchbox. "Sorry," she whispered.

"Don't be."

The first match flared, and Josh lit one of the lamps. Warm light bloomed across the kitchen, softer and more intimate than the overhead bulbs had been. He lit the second lamp, then started on the candles Alice had scattered across the table and counters.

"There." Alice surveyed her work with satisfaction. "Much better than fumbling around in the dark."

Katie had to agree. The flickering glow made everything feel different—quieter, more peaceful. Like they'd stepped into a different time.

Reaching for one of the flashlights, Josh looked to

Alice. "I'll check the breakers. Where's the panel box?"

"On the side of the house. Out the guest wing door, turn right. Only a few feet ahead."

"I'll come with you." Katie jumped to her feet. Not that she'd have a clue what to do with an electric panel, but…

Josh nodded and stretched his arm out, his fingers splayed in invitation.

Forcing herself to breathe steadily, she accepted his hand and almost forgot how to walk.

"While you two are checking the breakers, I'll call Clint." Alice reached for her cell phone. "Make sure the barn's okay and the water tanks are still working."

As if summoned by sheer will, the back door opened and Clint came in. "Glad to see the house generator is working." Stepping softly, he sidled up to Alice and gave her a quick peck on the lips, softly speaking, "You okay?"

Alice smiled up at him, her face softer than it had been with them. "Not my first blackout."

"No." He chuckled and kissed her on the tip of her nose.

"We're on our way to check the breakers." Josh gently squeezed her hand and Katie would have sworn in a court of law that all reasonable thought, including her own name, just leaked out her ears.

"Great. I'll grab a flashlight and head out to make sure the barn generator is working and check the water pumps. If it turns out to be the breaker box, I'll be back."

With one more quick kiss, Clint turned and walked out the back door as they walked down the rear hall. Content to have her hand held tightly in Josh's, Katie didn't mind admitting that if it meant getting to hold Josh's hand, she'd be perfectly happy if the lights never came back on. This was so not what she had expected from her visit to ranch country—seriously not what she'd expected.

CHAPTER FOURTEEN

The heavenly silence in the kitchen this morning was a welcome reprieve from the loud hum of the generator most of last night. Though Josh did need to thank whatever power company had blown the grid long enough for him to be able to walk hand in hand with Katie in search of the panel box. It was absolutely ludicrous how completely at peace and at home he felt with her hand in his. The warmth, the smallness enfolded in his large palm, the rhythmic sway of their arms with each step. He couldn't remember feeling so… good, so right, about… everything.

Leaning against the counter, Josh pulled out his cell phone. Alice and Clint had taken the truck into town early to pick up some much needed supplies. Maybe the tendency for all things ranch and all things military to start so blasted early in the morning was why being here had come so much more easily than he'd expected. From the corner of his eye he spotted Katie coming down the stairs. Then again, maybe early morning ranch life had nothing to do with his good mood.

"Hey man, what's up?" Kade's voice dragged his attention away from his love life, or potential love life, and back to the matter at hand.

In only a few minutes, he'd brought his buddy up to speed on yesterday's events at the pharmacy. "I'm telling you, Kade, he didn't even flinch. Luke had his arms wrapped around that dog's neck for so long I lost track of time. The kid was rocking and squeezing him tight. Raider just laid there and took it."

On the other end of the line, Kade let out a low whistle. "That's the restraint test, Josh. Most military working dogs fail that one because they see being held down as a threat. If he cleared that with a stranger—and a stressed-out kid at that—he's already ahead of the curve."

"That's what I'm thinking." Josh straightened, testing his balance. Solid. No spin. "So, what's next? If I want to prove to whoever matters that he's therapy dog material, what do I need to determine?"

"Therapy dogs isn't my specialty, but there are some basics that you should check. First, recovery from startle. Drop a metal pan behind him. See if he recovers or goes into defense mode. And obedience transfer. He listens to you, and he listens to me, but a therapy dog has to listen to the handler in charge, even if that person changes."

"Got it."

"Most important is to stay aware of him. He may have been great with Luke yesterday, but he's trained to bite bad guys. Don't set him up to fail."

"I won't."

The floorboards creaked and Josh turned to find Katie stepping into the kitchen. Dressed in jeans and a flannel shirt, her hair pulled back in that messy ponytail, she somehow managed to look better than any woman he'd ever seen.

She smiled, pointing to the coffee pot.

"I've got to run, Kade." Josh watched her pour two mugs. "I'll call back later to keep you posted."

"Roger that. Stay safe."

Katie turned, extending a mug. "Black."

"Thanks." He smiled. Their fingers brushed briefly, reminding him once again of how right it felt last night in the dark. "That was Kade. I was picking his brain about Raider."

"Does he agree with us about therapy work?"

"Could be." Josh set the mug down on the counter. "Kade gave me a list of how to test his suitability for the job. We've already unintentionally done the hug test with Luke."

Katie sipped her coffee, looking over the rim, and nodded.

"The testing is a two man job. Care to help me run him through his paces?"

Setting her mug down beside his, a smile bloomed. "I'd love to."

Ten minutes later, they were out on the flat stretch of grass between the house and the barn. He clipped a long lead onto Raider's collar. The dog stood instantly, shaking off his nap, his posture shifting from pet to soldier the moment the leash clicked. "Okay," Josh handed her the end of the leather lead, "take him."

Katie reached out, grabbing the strap loosely in her fist.

"Not like that." Josh moved behind her. "If he takes off, he'll pull that right out of your grip."

Determination etched on her face, she nodded.

He stepped in close. Reaching around her, he covered her hands with his own. Swallowing hard, he forced himself to focus despite the hint of vanilla in her hair. "Loop your thumb here." He guided her fingers, feeling a slight hitch in her breath beneath his hands—or maybe that was his own. "Keep your arm relaxed but ready."

"Like this?" she whispered, leaning back slightly against his chest.

"Perfect." Josh forced himself to release her hands and take a much needed step back. "Now, stand tall. Shoulders back. Dogs read body language. Tell him *heel* and walk toward the fence. Low voice. Firm."

Katie squared her shoulders. "Raider, heel."

To Josh's pride—and relief—Raider looked up at Katie, fell into step beside her and walked with a perfect, rhythmic gait.

"Look at that," Josh called out, watching them move away. "He's listening to you."

Katie beamed. Turning her head to smile at him over her shoulder, she gave him a thumbs up with her free hand.

"Don't let it go to your head." Josh jogged lightly to catch up. "Next test may be more of a challenge. The startle."

"The startle. Do I want to know what that entails?" Her tone was half-teasing, half-concern and as adorable as all get out.

At the water trough he picked up an empty metal feed bucket. "Walk him away from me. When I drop this, don't react. Just keep walking like the noise is no big deal. We'll see if he can ignore a falling tray in a hospital or if he'll respond to a threat in fight mode."

Katie nodded, her gaze focused and intense. "Raider, heel."

Josh waited a few moments, then tossed the metal bucket against the trough with a loud *CLANG*. In the quiet pasture the sound, as intended, was jarring. Raider spun around, ears pinned back, his body tense. Josh held his breath.

Katie slowed. She didn't yank the leash. She just looked down at the dog, her voice calm and steady. "It's okay, Raider."

Raider stared in the direction of the noise for one second, two. Then his ears relaxed and he looked up at Katie, waiting for direction.

"Yes." Josh punched the air.

Grinning wild and bright, Katie turned, dropped the leash, ran toward Josh, and reached out to high-five him. Their hands met with a solid smack, but instead of pulling away, Josh caught her hand.

He interlaced their fingers.

"We did it," she nearly whispered, her face flushed from the excitement or his touch, but he had no clue which.

The warmth of Josh's hand encompassing hers sent a sharp jolt of awareness straight to Katie's toes. For a suspended moment, with heat warming her cheeks, she forgot about the training, the furlough, and the fact that Josh held her hand to celebrate a dog not attacking a bucket.

Apparently feeling left out of the team huddle, Raider nudged his weight against them, breaking the spell.

Josh chuckled and slowly—to her chagrin—released

her fingers. "Okay. Valid point, Raider. We aren't done yet."

"What's next?" Katie tucked a loose strand of hair behind her ear, trying to give her hand something to do besides snatch his back.

"The crowding test." Josh clipped the leash back onto Raider's collar. "Kade calls it the 'Clumsy Stranger.' A therapy dog has to be bombproof. People in hospitals or nursing homes move unpredictably. They shuffle, they trip, they drop things, and they encroach on personal space. Raider has to hold his sit-stay no matter what."

"And I'm the clumsy stranger?"

"You're the actress." Josh's eyes twinkled. "I need you to walk past him, but not in a straight line. Weave a little. Bump his shoulder with your leg. Maybe stumble toward him. We need to make sure he doesn't interpret that physical contact as an attack."

"So, basically walk like I've had too much of the punch at the Sweet family Christmas party?"

"Exactly."

Josh reset the dog. "Raider, sit. Stay."

The dog dropped his haunches, his gaze locked on Josh. The intensity of the animal straddled something between terrifying and beautiful. She just hoped beautiful won out when she bumped him.

"Action," Josh called out.

Exaggerating her walk, she felt utterly ridiculous. Drifting aimlessly to the left and then correcting sharply to the right, she headed straight for the dog. Katie let her hip check the dog's shoulder as she stumbled past. It wasn't a hard hit, but enough to knock a smaller dog off balance.

Raider shifted his weight to absorb the bump, let out a huff of air, and looked up at Katie with an expression that clearly read, *What the heck?* But he didn't growl. He didn't break his sit.

"Good boy." Josh praised, tossing a treat. He looked at Katie. "Again. This time come at him from the front."

They ran the drill three more times. Katie stomped, swayed, and invaded the dog's personal bubble. Every time,

Raider held his ground, looking to Josh for reassurance and receiving it.

Watching Josh work was a revelation. In the kitchen, he was soft—gentle smiles and quiet conversation. Out here, in *handler mode,* he was different. His shoulders were squared, his voice dropped an octave, commanding but never harsh. He moved with an efficiency that made her realize just how much effort he must have been putting into simply walking straight for the last two weeks.

"He's solid," Josh declared, scrubbing Raider's neck with affection. "I think Kade is going to be surprised."

"I think *you* are the one surprising people." Katie walked over to join them.

Josh looked up, shielding his eyes from the sun. "How so?"

"Look at you." She gestured to him. "You've been out here spinning, bending down, handling a powerhouse dog, and you haven't reached for a fence post once."

Josh paused. He looked down at his feet, then back at her, a realization dawning on his face. "I guess I haven't."

"You're getting your sea legs back, soldier."

"Maybe I just have a good spotter," he countered, his gaze holding hers.

"Okay, flattery will get you everywhere." She laughed, turning toward the house. "But I think this is more than enough for one day."

"Agreed. Let's head in."

They started the trek back across the pasture. The ground here was rougher than the manicured lawn near the house—clumps of crabgrass, and uneven ruts from the ranch vehicles and cattle.

"So now what?" Katie asked.

"Now that we have power again, I'll do a search on what steps are required for a therapy dog."

"I wonder if Sara Sue would know?"

Josh bobbed his head. "I should have thought of that."

"I'm sure you would have." Paying more attention to the strong gait of the man and his dog—because whether he knew it or not, Raider was now his dog—the toe of her boot caught the lip of a dry rut. It happened fast. One second she was walking, the next gravity took over. Her ankle rolled, and she pitched forward with a sharp gasp.

"Whoa!" Josh's voice was deep and low and before she could hit the dirt, a steel band clamped around her waist. Josh caught her, hauling her upright, pulling her flush against his chest to steady her.

Katie's hands flew up, landing on his biceps. The muscle beneath her palms was rock hard. She waited for the sway. She expected him to stumble, for the sudden movement to trigger his dizziness. But he didn't move. He was rooted to the spot, holding her weight and his own without a tremor.

His face was inches from hers, his eyes dark and intense. He didn't let go. "You okay?"

"I'm fine," she muttered. "You seem to be doing better yourself, I, on the other hand, think I failed the walking test."

"I think you passed the trust test."

He held her for a beat longer than necessary, the air between them charged. For a fraction of a second she thought maybe—*hoped* maybe—he was going to kiss her. Then slowly, regretfully, he loosened his grip, letting her find her feet and took a long step in retreat.

"Thanks." She smoothed her shirt, her heart hammering against her ribs.

"Anytime." His voice was low and rough and made her skin tingle.

It took a moment for her to fall into step beside Josh and Raider; this time, she kept her eyes on the ground. She wasn't sure she'd survive another rescue if she tripped again.

They'd just reached the back porch when Josh's phone rang. "I bet that's Kade checking up on how it went." Instead of answering, his gaze narrowed on the phone.

"What's wrong?"

He shook his head. "Odd. It's not Kade, it's Alice." Tapping the phone and hitting speaker, he took the call. "Hey, Ms. Sweet. What's up?"

CHAPTER FIFTEEN

"We have a situation. I need your help. ASAP." Alice Sweet's voice came through the phone's speaker loud and clear and laced with panic.

Instinctively, Josh picked up his pace. Katie had to hasten her step to keep up. He'd never heard that tone in Alice's voice before.

"It's Luke."

The little boy from yesterday. Could it be another meltdown? Did they need Raider? His mind raced ahead to gathering the dog, finding the keys to the other truck as he hurried toward the back porch.

"He's gone." Alice's words came through hard and cold.

Josh jolted to a stop, staring down at the phone. "Gone, how?"

In front of him, Katie paused, her hand coming to rest on his forearm holding the phone, worry painted on her face and in her eyes.

"They never found his lovie. His mom and dad thought it was fine after Raider calmed him down, but last night Luke kept asking for his baseball bear lovie. When he drifted off to sleep without it, they thought all was well. Until this morning."

Katie squeezed her eyes shut. Her thoughts probably going to the same place his had. This morning. Last night. There were a lot of hours in between and Luke was so... defenseless.

"The whole town has been alerted, but Luke is noise sensitive. People roaming around screaming his name is only going to make him hide, not come out."

Already on the porch, in two long strides, he yanked at the screen door so hard, he almost pulled the hinges out. This entire time, Katie was to one side of him, Raider on the other. His gaze dropped to the dog. Once a military dog, always a military dog. Raider could sense trouble just the same as everyone else.

"We need Brady." Only the slight crack in her voice told Josh just how frantic Ms. Alice was over the little boy. "He can find him. Get him here as fast as you can."

Of course. Like Raider, Brady was trained to track and find weapons, ammunition, bombs. Give him a scent of a boy and he'd probably find him the same way he'd uncovered Cassie in training the other day.

"We don't have search and rescue teams here and it will take too long for help to arrive from any of the big cities. Brady's our best bet."

"Agreed." What Josh didn't know was who the heck was going to handle the animal? He had observed enough of the search part of the K9 team but he didn't have a clue about the rescue part.

Inside, Katie had already gone to where the leads were hanging in the back hall.

"Does he still have a work halter? A vest?" Josh knew that Brady would understand he was being put to work, but the vest would signal this wasn't training, this was the real deal.

"Of course," Alice sighed. "I should have thought of that. There's a cabinet next to where we keep the leashes and collars. His old vest is hanging inside."

Bless Katie. She'd have made a great soldier. No waiting for instructions, she was already opening the cabinet and pulling out the vest. Without being told, she'd pulled out her own phone and was calling Benny, the head ranch hand. As Alice explained where to bring Brady, he could hear Katie telling Benny to get Brady back to the ranch faster than the speed of light.

"And Josh?"

"Yes?"

"Hurry. His mom is inconsolable." Alice didn't have to state the obvious. Depending on where the child had gone, there were too many places, too many ways for the kid to be in serious danger. The late night cold snaps this time of year was their first hurdle. He didn't want to think about predators, and prayed the kid hadn't been out alone all night.

Taking a minute, Josh strode quickly to his room, Katie on his heels. Inside, he went to his lock box, pulled out his handgun and holster. The sound of Katie's gasp had him stopping short, the gun in one hand and holster in the other. "There's no telling what we'll find out there."

Her hands on her mouth, Katie's head bobbed up and down, her eyes wide with fear and yet, he could see the wheels turning in the back of her mind, the understanding of all a lost child in the West Texas landscape could entail.

Quickly, he clipped the holster and gun inside his waistband and strapped a knife to his calf. Knowing there was no time to spare, but seeing how raw the weapons had left Katie, he pulled her into a quick embrace. "We'll find him. It will be okay. He's probably tucked away in a quiet place just waiting for us to find him."

Her head in his shoulder, she nodded, sucked in a deep breath, and pulled back, drawing from a strength he hadn't expected to see. Should have, but hadn't. "I know, it's just the city girl in me that was a little surprised, and trying very hard not to think of what dangers could be out there."

Gently, he ran the back of his knuckles under her chin, shoving the same visions of a hurt little boy out of his head. "We've got this."

Another deep breath and she retreated another step. "You need to hurry."

A few feet down the hall, Raider was seated patiently under the line of hanging leashes.

The sight brought a half-hearted twitch to corners of his mouth. Not really a smile, but quite the sight.

"I think Raider wants to come too."

Josh shook his head. "We don't know what we're up against. He's not strong enough yet."

The dog shifted his sit, stared at Josh, and for a second there he could almost hear the dog threatening Josh if he left without him.

At that moment, Benny blew through the back door, Brady at his side. "Here he is. Interesting dog. All I said is there's a boy in trouble, and I'd swear he understood."

Josh nodded. "No swearing. I'm sure he understands." Brady had been one of the best K9s he'd ever worked with. The animal had saved his and others in his team's lives more than once. A slight whine—not quite a whimper, more of a dog's version of clearing his throat—came from Raider, reminding Josh he was ready and able too. "All right. You both come. But you," he pointed to Raider, "stay with Katie until you're needed."

Katie's one brow shot high on her forehead. "Did he just nod at you?"

Leads hooked on the two collars, Josh lifted his gaze to meet hers. "Probably. Now let's go find a little boy."

The drive to the Millers' home just outside of town had seemed to take an eternity. As they passed through town, people could be seen, much like the other day, wandering around looking down alleys, scattered about the park, the playground, in and around neighbors' yards and fences and so far nothing on the boy or his treasured security blanket.

The Miller's home had become a command post. Police from neighboring towns had joined the search. Organized in grids, concerned friends, strangers, everyone scavenged carefully for any signs of Luke. Wide vacant prairie spread out around the homestead, neighbors and officers, at double arm's length, meticulously searched every inch of ground.

Josh pulled the truck to a stop by the tables set up in the front yard. Alice Sweet reached the truck before anyone could finish descending. Katie kept a tight grip on Raider's leash, Josh had control of Brady. The dog, still highly trained, stood firm, tense, waiting for his instructions.

Katherine Miller, Luke's mother, came running from inside the house. "Thank you!" she shouted at Josh, her pained expression squeezing at his heart like a vise. "This is his pillow and his jacket. I wasn't sure which would be better." She sucked in a deep breath. "If we still had it I would give you his lovie, but we don't." The poor woman was clearly holding it together by a very thin thread.

"The jacket will work." Josh took it from her hand, and held it in front of Brady. "Take a good sniff boy. We need to find Luke."

The dog sniffed. Looked up at Josh then sniffed the jacket again. Katie held her breath, hoping this worked. Another second and Brady lifted his nose to the air and took off, practically dragging Josh across the yard.

"I knew it," Alice almost cheered then turned to the mother. "It's going to be all right. I know it."

"I'd better keep up." Katie tightened her grip on Raider and trotted over to Josh's side, praying Jackie's mother-in-law was right. "Alice told Mrs. Miller that Brady's going to find Luke."

"I heard." His focus remained on the ground and the dog. The way the muscles in his jaw twitched, she'd bet he was as worried as she was that Mrs. Sweet may have made promises none of them could keep.

Moving at twice, maybe three times the pace that a little boy could wander, especially if, like a normal boy distractions slowed him down, Josh and Katie followed Brady's lead. By the time they'd left the Miller property it was just the two of them following Brady as the rest of the search crew fanned out in other directions.

With every passing minute, the wind had picked up, whistling through the scrub brush with a low, mournful howl that masked the sounds they desperately needed to hear.

"Keep your eyes on the ground." Josh moved just ahead of her, his flashlight beam sweeping the terrain. On a long lead ahead of him, Brady kept his nose to the dirt, moving with a grim determination.

Walking for over an hour, Katie worried about Raider.

The animal's determination was mind boggling. For all she knew, he was hurting like hell but that wasn't going to stop him. Suddenly, with Josh only a few steps in front of her, Raider froze. The hairs on his neck rose and the animal lunged forward, almost dragging Katie with him.

She heard rather than saw what had the dog riled up. The shaking sound of a baby's rattle out in the middle of the West Texas prairie had the hair on Katie's arms standing on end. Coiled in the deep grass—only a few feet away from them—a rattlesnake. One decisive *crack* split the air. The snake's body jerked, then went limp and her knees almost did the same.

Beside her now, Josh holstered the weapon and reached for her hand, his thumb brushing hers. "You okay?"

She nodded, though her heart was rattling louder than that snake ever could have.

"And *that* is why I grabbed my gun."

All she could do was nod once more. Sometime later when she found her voice, she'd say thank you.

They pushed deeper into a small canyon. Brady stopped, sniffing frantically at a cluster of mesquite bushes. Josh crouched down. "Hold up."

Katie moved closer, shining her light where Josh pointed. In the dirt, perfectly preserved, was a massive paw print. Too big for a dog. No claw marks.

"Mountain lion," Josh murmured.

Marvelous. As if snakes weren't enough of a threat for a lost little boy, now they had mountain lions to contend with. Her gaze followed Brady. Snagged on a thorny branch, fluttering in the wind, a scrap of blue and white fabric had captured the dog's attention. "The lovie."

"He was here," Josh whispered, his gaze carefully surveying their surroundings.

"And the lion?"

Josh shook his head. "No idea if these are fresh or old tracks. For all I know, Luke was never here and it was the lion who found and carried off the small blanket."

If it were up to her, she'd vote for old tracks and Luke would be nearby. But then again, if she had any say in life, everyone, including Luke, would be home safe and warm in their homes. Trudging forward, she had to hold on to that vision, everyone safe and sound in their homes. Including little Luke. She just had to.

CHAPTER SIXTEEN

Exhaustion had begun to set in. Katie's legs felt heavier with every step. Even Raider, though determined to continue, was favoring his bad leg. More than once Katie considered it might be time to take the poor dog home, but every time she opened her mouth to broach the subject with Josh, Raider looked at her with big soulful eyes that seemed to be pleading with her to let him keep looking. A small part of her would have argued the dog had no idea why they were here or who they were looking for; after all, he had not sniffed Luke's jacket as Brady had, but looking in his eyes, no one was going to convince her that the dog was not fully aware of exactly what was going on—and what the stakes were. So they pushed on.

When she wasn't watching Josh, the dogs, or the horizon, she looked over her shoulder. After she'd told Alice that they'd found the lovie, the family matriarch had texted that backup was coming to help search that area. That was over half an hour ago.

"The sun is beginning to set." She'd just stated the obvious, but there was no ignoring how the sun was hanging lower in the sky already.

Josh stopped. "I hate to think of him spending another night out here alone."

She couldn't agree more. Texts had been bouncing back and forth, search teams reporting little other than where Luke was not hiding. Even though more people were coming their way, no one was giving up anywhere else. But as long as Brady still had a scent to follow, backup or not, neither she nor Josh, nor the dogs, were ready to give up.

Moving forward, keeping her eyes out for more snakes or, heaven forbid, the mountain lion, Brady alerted. His ears pointed forward, his nose twitched, and he gave a low sharp bark, loud enough to announce, not so loud to alarm Luke. How the dog knew that she did not understand, but she was glad as heck for it. Brady pulled toward a dark opening in a crop of rocks ahead. She had no idea there were caves out here. Only as they got closer did they realize this was not an organic cave. The beam of the flashlight revealed rotted timber framing and a rusted metal sign that hung crookedly from a post: DANGER. KEEP OUT.

Josh shone his light into the gloom. "Looks like an abandoned mine."

"You think he went in there?" If he did, that poor kid had to be scared to death.

"It's a shelter from the wind. And if that cat was stalking him…" Josh didn't finish the sentence. He unclipped Brady's leash. "I'm going in. You stay here."

He might have been talking to her, but Brady was having none of it. Pressing against Josh's leg, he poked at the lead with his nose.

"All right." Josh heaved a sigh. "I suppose if anyone knows how to walk gingerly it would be you, boy." He looked up at her. "You two stay here. If I find anything I'll let you know."

"I don't like it." Every internal alarm she had was going off. If she'd been on an old sci-fi television show there'd be a robot shouting *Danger, Josh, danger*. "It does not look very stable."

He shook his head. "No, it doesn't. But if Luke is in there, we don't have a choice."

She couldn't argue with that. Not sure what possessed her, but she lurched forward, grabbed hold of his arm, leaned in, and gave him a good hard kiss on the lips. "Be careful."

Eyes wide, he stared for a moment before a hint of a smile tugged at the corners of his mouth. "You too."

Her gaze remained on him until they disappeared into the black mouth of the shaft. Raider pulled at her, twisting at the end of the leash. "Take it easy, boy. They're okay."

The dog did not like what she had to say. He continued to tug and twist and was actually trying to wiggle his way out of the leash.

Pulling out her phone, she shot Alice a text about the cave.

Alice texted back: *Should be at your location in a few minutes.*

Katie stood staring at the dark hole, straining to hear anything over the wind. Counting the minutes down on her watch, wondering if Josh could send a text inside that shaft.

Leaves crumpled behind her and instantly Alice appeared with Clint at her side. "Any luck?"

She shook her head. "They've been in there for almost ten minutes…" A low rumble echoed from somewhere inside the mine and Katie's head snapped around. The ground beneath her feet vibrated, followed by a sickening *CRACK.*

"Josh!"

No answer, followed by a roaring rumble. Plumes of dust and smoke billowed from the entrance.

"Oh my God!" She ran forward, but Raider blocked her path, his body a wall. "Josh!"

No answer. Rocks slid down the canyon wall, burying the entrance in a pile of rubble and timber.

This time Alice screamed, her voice tumbling over Clint's and Katie's. "Josh! Josh, answer me!"

The three ran toward the pile. Coughing, she and Clint clawed at the rocks with bare hands. Alice had the sheriff on the phone calling for more help. Luke may or may not be inside, but now they had Josh and Brady to rescue.

Alice's next call was to her son Carson. "We've had an accident."

"I heard. Sheriff already called. Hardware store is on their way with lumber. Keep everyone away until I can get there and shore the shaft up. If it's the one I'm thinking, that sucker is probably held up by beams turned to dust."

Katie didn't care what she'd overheard, she was not stopping. She had to reach Josh. He had to be okay.

Within minutes, organized chaos ensued. Men brought two-by-fours from the trucks. Carson barked orders about load-bearing rocks. People were carefully pulling debris away, but every time they moved a stone, the earth groaned. And then…*CRACK*. Another plume of dust shot out.

"Get back! Everyone back!" Carson roared.

The rescuers scrambled away as more rock shifted. Katie stood frozen, her eyes fixed on the pile of rubble that had become a tomb. She felt a hand on her shoulder. Alice stood at her side, her face white as a sheet, but her grip solid.

"He's okay," Alice whispered, though her voice shook. "He has to be."

Katie leaned into the older woman, watching the dust settle. A bitter thought clawed at her throat. Josh had survived multiple tours in the sandbox. He had survived IEDs and ambushes. She didn't want to think how that's the way it always happened. Good men survived multiple deployments to war zones only to trip on a bar of soap and crack their skulls open. She reached down blindly to scratch Raider's ears, needing the comfort of the animal. Her hand met empty air. Katie looked down. The leash was trailing on the ground. "Raider?"

She spun around. "Where's Raider?"

The frantic energy of the rescue site paused. One of the men working on the lumber supports stretched out his arm. "The gray dog? He bolted that way a minute ago. I thought he was chasing a rabbit."

Without thinking, she grabbed a flashlight and ran in the direction the hand pointed. If she couldn't dig out Josh and Brady, she was damned if she was going to lose Raider. Hurrying through the tall grass, pushing any fears of snakes out of her mind, she searched for any sign of the newly missing dog. Exhaustion and desperation taking over, she slowed, came to a stop, leaned over, her hands on her knees, her eyes closed as she gathered the strength to keep going. Fighting back tears, she sucked in a deep breath, straightened her back, and looked to the sky. "Oh, Josh."

"You rang?"

Spinning around to where the deep voice came from, she found Josh covered in dust, cradling a small boy against his chest, with a dog seated at either side of him.

She didn't dare move. If this was a dream, she didn't want to break the spell.

Of all the times Josh had been caught in a less than positive situation where he had thought he was surely going to buy the farm and meet his buddies in heaven, being trapped in a collapsing mine had definitely moved to the top of his list. Never had he been so happy as to see Raider inching toward them from the opposite direction, or happy that he'd followed the smart dog.

Only when he heard Katie calling his name to the heavens as he reached the light of day, did it truly sink in that this time, he was not going to die.

Standing in front of him, mouth open, hands clasped in front of her, Katie wasn't moving, wasn't speaking.

Zipping around him, Raider bolted to where she stood and wiggling around like a dog much younger and healthier than him, he barked at Katie.

Down on her haunches, she blinked, pet the scruff of the dog's neck, leveled her gaze with Josh and slowly opened her mouth. "You're real."

"Last time I checked, yeah." Now, he stood in front of her. "I hope that's okay."

Katie sprang to her feet, and carefully placing her hand on Luke's back, smiled up at Josh. "Better than okay."

"You had me scared for a minute."

"I had you scared? Are you kidding? I've never been more afraid of losing someone I loved in my entire life."

"Well, if you put it that way…" his words suddenly clogged in his throat as his brain fully processed what she'd said. "Wait. You love me?"

Her cheeks flushed, she took a step back, and nibbling on her lower lip, slowly nodded.

If it were possible for a human heart to burst with joy, his was pretty dang close. "Does this mean it's okay to mention that I love you?"

"You do?" She inched closer again.

He nodded, and Luke pulled away from the crook of his neck. "Mama."

"Mama!" Katie threw her hands in the air. "I'd better let Alice know."

"No need." Alice trotted up to them, Clint on her heels, his phone at his ear. "Well, young man," she stopped at Josh's side, "*you* are a sight for sore eyes."

Clint gently placed a blanket on Luke. "How's he doing?"

"Doesn't seem to have any issues. I think he was in the mine most of the night. No sign of animal tracks in the mine. I didn't notice any bruises or injuries and he doesn't feel warm or cold, so I think he's going to be all right."

"We have Doc Conroy on his way anyhow." Alice gently patted Luke's back, pulling her hand away when the boy snuggled deeper into Josh's shoulder.

The crowd grew. Luke's mother appeared, her husband at her side, and practically ripped her son from Josh's arms. Another moment later and the doc showed up. Cheers and high fives made their rounds all the way back to the Miller's yard. The command post dismantled, the volunteers making their way back to town or home, Doc Conroy giving Luke a clean bill of health, Josh walked Katie to the truck. Opening the back door, the two dogs gingerly climbed in and settled in the back seat.

Josh closed the door behind the dogs and turned to Katie. "Back to the ranch?"

Nodding, rather than step up into the truck, she stepped into his personal space.

With an ease he hadn't expected, Josh wrapped his arms around her. "I meant what I said. I love you."

"Me too."

"You love you too?" he teased.

Chuckling, she tipped her head back to meet his gaze. "I love you too. Now the question is, what are we going to do about this?"

CHAPTER SEVENTEEN

"All right. I think today's effort calls for everyone's favorite lasagna." Pulling open the freezer door, Alice Sweet pulled out a foil covered aluminum pan almost as big as she was.

"Here," Josh jumped up from his seat and reached his friend's mother before the weight of the pan toppled her over, "I've got this."

She smiled up at him, an unusual glint in her eyes. "Thank you."

When she continued to grin at him without moving or closing the freezer door, he had to ask. "What? Do I still have dirt on my face?"

"You're not careful anymore." As if that explained everything, she bumped the freezer closed and maneuvered around him. "Set that on the stove and I'll see what else I can rustle up."

The back door blew open and in stomped Preston and Sara Sue with Carson and Jessica right behind them.

"Just so you know," Sara Sue dropped her purse on an empty chair, "Katherine Miller is planning on supplying Raider and Brady with steaks for the rest of their lives. Luke is not only home and happy, he's decided Raider is his new best friend."

"They deserve it." Alice returned to the freezer.

"I'll second that." Katie reached over and scratched Raider's ear. At her feet, the dog swished his tail once then twice before dozing off again.

Moving to sit beside Katie before someone else took the spot, he sat. Stretching his arm out, he snatched her hand in his, delighted when their fingers laced together. For the next few moments, he had no idea what anyone else had said. The adrenaline from the day was still rushing through his system, topped off by Katie's declaration, and he didn't think he'd ever come off the mountaintop high. Katie Lawford loved him.

While more family members arrived, making the din of conversation rise with each new addition around the massive table, Josh's phone sounded. For one long moment he was tempted to let the call go to voicemail, but reluctantly letting go of Katie's hand, he pushed to his feet, and phone to his ear, made his way outside. "Hello."

"I heard you and the dogs are heroes."

"How far does the Honeysuckle grapevine go?"

Kade barked a sharp laugh. "At least to the base. I've been getting updates from pretty much everyone in the family all day, including my aunts Liz and Vicki."

"I'll remember that if I ever want to keep a secret." Which right about now he was pretty sure would be damn near impossible anywhere within a hundred mile radius of the Sweet Ranch.

"As long as we're talking updates, Mom tells me your vertigo is gone."

"Why would she say that?" His mind drifted back to her comment by the freezer, *he wasn't careful anymore.*

"Is she wrong?"

Was she? He'd been able to nod and shake his head for a while now, and as he thought on it, he realized, he really had stopped being careful. He actually could not remember the last time he had to steady himself against a wall, or extend his arms to catch his balance. "I don't know."

He could almost hear Kade rolling his eyes through the phone connection. "Of course you do."

Yeah, maybe he did. "I've got a checkup with the doc in a couple of days, I'll report back."

"So, if you get a clean bill of health, does that mean you'll be back on base driving the soldiers crazy?"

Did it? Would he? "I guess."

Silence hung for several long seconds. "You guess?"

"Truth?"

"Always."

"I'm not sure. There have been some other changes."

"Katie?"

"How did you know?"

"You're kidding, right?" Kade heaved a sigh. "It was pretty obvious when I was home that there was a little chemistry bouncing off the walls whenever y'all were in the same room, and according to Cassie—"

"Ah," he cut Kade off, "your inside man."

Again, Kade laughed out loud. "Something like that."

"Not to cut you short, but any updates on Kent or Boglioli?"

"Coming along. Boglioli should be released from rehab any day now."

"That's what he said when I spoke to him earlier this week. He mentioned needing more PT."

"Yeah. He can walk now, but with the limp, he wouldn't be able to carry a pack or pass a physical for duty. He'll need intensive therapy to correct that."

"I see."

"I hear the wheels turning."

Josh laughed, so maybe his buddy wasn't as good a mind reader as he gave him credit for. "Let me look into a few things and I'll get back to you."

"Fair enough." In the background a sharp dog bark could be heard, followed by the muffled sound of voices as Kade must have placed his hand over the phone. "Listen. Sorry to call and run, but we got a situation here. Take care of yourself and let me know what the doc says."

"Will do." The call disconnected and staring out into the dark distance, he asked himself the same question that Kade had. Today, after everything, he knew he could go back in the military if he wanted to. The question at hand now though wasn't if he could, but did he want to?

Lightly tapping her nails on the tabletop, Katie kept one eye on Josh outside while recapping for the umpteenth time about finding the mine, the cave in, and the happy ending for little Luke. When the conversation shifted to the smell of fresh baked bread that Alice had taken from freezer to oven, noticing that Josh had placed his phone back into his pocket with no sign of coming back inside, she opted to join him outside. "Hey, there."

His back to her, Josh turned at the sound of her voice. A sweet smile on his face. "Hi there." He extended his arm to her.

Accepting his hand, she was almost surprised when he tugged her in close, nestling her against him.

Looping his arms around her waist, the smile slipped and heat seemed to fuel the intensity of his gaze. "I hope you don't mind."

She shook her head.

"Good." Pulling her even closer, his lips touched hers. Softly at first, then harder and sweeter until she was pretty sure her toes had curled in her shoes.

Was it crazy for her to wish she could stay here just like this, on the back porch, in his arms, with a blanket of stars shining down on them forever? A scratching noise followed by the squeaking hinges of the screen door had her easing away.

Instead of one of the family, Raider had pushed his way onto the porch with them.

"You trying to cut into my action?" Josh teased the dog now seated between them.

"Seems more like a chaperone to me."

The fingers of Josh's hand once again entwined with hers, he tugged her around the dog and over to his side so they were both leaning against the railing. "This is nice."

"Having a chaperone?" She smiled.

"Us. Here. Together. If I didn't make myself clear earlier, I love you. And not like a sister or my best friend's little sister, I am card carrying in love with you, Katie Lawford."

These words from any other man might have scared her half to death. An only child raised by a single mom, she didn't do relationships well. Not long term ones. But now, here, with this man, the guy who had gotten under her skin from almost day one. She didn't have a doubt in the world how she felt for him. "I can assure you, I do not love you like a brother."

That had them both laughing.

Lifting her hand so they were in both of his, he softly caressed her hand with his thumb. "I've been thinking."

Her heart sputtered to a stop, unsure if the next words were going to be gloriously good, or devastatingly dismal.

"I could stay in the army, but I've already done my twenty. I don't have to stay. Not anymore."

Now her heart had kick-started itself and was pounding rapidly against her ribs. "I thought you loved your life in the military?"

"I do. Did. But nothing I do for Uncle Sam compares to being with you. I don't want to lose you. Us."

She shook her head. "Neither do I."

His gaze dropped down to Raider. "Though I think we're a package deal."

"Absolutely." She smiled down at the dog. "I'm not sure if we're going to adopt him, or if he's already adopted us."

"Us." Josh leaned in and kissed her temple. "I really really like the sound of that."

"You know," she tried not to be lost in the sensation of tender lips against her skin, "I could leave my job if you'd rather stay in the army."

"But you like your job."

"I do. But it's a job. Not my life."

"You'd do that for me?" Now he kissed the tip of her nose.

Eyes closed, she slowly bobbed her chin.

"I think we have more to discuss, don't we?"

She nodded again. "But for tonight, it's enough to know I'm more important than Uncle Sam."

"Let's agree on one thing." He shifted to stand in front of her, his fingers gently tucking a lock of hair behind her ear. "Whatever we do next, from now on, we do it together."

"Mm, together."

"After all, we do make a good team."

"That we do." Raising her arms to drape around his neck, she leaned in for another soul stealing kiss, then sighed. "A very good team."

EPILOGUE

"**M**an, those two look happy." Sitting in a seat by Aiden's bed in the rehab facility, Kade Sweet flipped through another photo on his phone.

"You sure about that?" Aiden Boglioli couldn't believe that his love 'em and leave 'em staff sergeant had been bitten by the happily ever after bug.

"See for yourself." Staff Sergeant Kade Sweet handed Aiden his phone.

Studying the first photo, Aiden let out a long whistle. "Wow, she's a looker."

"Careful," Kade chuckled, "Josh is very protective of Katie."

"Can't say that I blame him. If a woman like that loved me, I'd be pretty darn protective of her too." He swiped at the screen, glancing at one picture after the other, studying some longer than others. Whether the couple was posing for the photo or caught in a candid shot, these two people oozed love.

Aiden wasn't what people would call lucky in love, but he knew it when he saw it in other people. And these two had that look down pat. The sparkle in their eyes. The grins on their faces. The way in every photo, no matter who was the centerpiece, Josh and Katie could be seen staring at each other from across the room, or across the table. As if they couldn't stand to be apart.

Actually, as he took his time going from one photo after another, he noticed that a lot of the couples in these pictures seemed to have that same gleam in their eyes. Maybe it was a Texas thing.

"So," Kade leaned back in the sleek chair, "how's the therapy going?"

"Fine." Aiden continued to swipe. He was fascinated by all the couples in all the photos, especially the staff sergeant and his new girl. Though from the looks of it all, Aiden was pretty sure this lady would become a more permanent fixture in his sergeant's life sooner than later.

"Just fine?"

Aiden shrugged. "Doctors are happy. Nurses too. Therapists, it's hard to read." He was supposed to be released days ago, but there had been some glitches with his paperwork.

"Any word on what's next after they let you out of this place?"

That was a good question. So far his rehab had gone well, at least that's what the docs were saying. He just wished he felt more like himself. He didn't like being broken, even if the doctor only called it a fracture. Anything that required hospitals, rehab, and PT should be called something stronger than a fracture in his mind. Especially when it left him with such a pronounced limp. "I suppose as soon as they figure out who dropped the ball with the paperwork."

He swiped through more photos. Pictures of Josh and his lady in front of cows, and horses, and gardens, and fixing what Aiden was pretty sure were fence posts. After all, even a New York City boy like himself should be able to recognize what fence repair looked like.

"Have they at least given you options?"

He wanted to respond, but the problem was, no one had yet to give him a straight answer. There were always different things to consider, contemplate, and just plain fudge around. So the fast and easy answer was that he didn't have a clue where he was going next, but he was sure of one thing, if his gait didn't improve, finding a new home in the army didn't appear to be very likely.

At that moment, Kade's phone rang.

Retrieving his phone, Kade glanced down at the Caller ID, and pushing to his feet, he lifted a finger at Aiden. "I'll take this in the hall. Regulations."

"Hey there, buddy. How are the love birds doing?"

Assuming Josh and Katie were the only lovebirds Kade knew, Aiden had to shake his head. Who'd have thunk his staff sergeant would fall head over boot heels in love. *Wouldn't that be nice.*

MEET CHRIS

USA TODAY Bestselling Author of dozens of contemporary novels, including the award winning Aloha Series, Chris Keniston lives in suburban Dallas with her husband, two human children, and two canine children. Though she loves her puppies equally, she admits being especially attached to her German Shepherd rescue. After all, even dogs deserve a happily ever after.

More on Chris and all her books can be found at
www.chriskeniston.com

Follow Chris' Monday Blog at her website
ChrisKenistonAuthor

Follow Chris on Facebook at
ChrisKenistonAuthor

Never miss a New Release!
Sign up for News from Chris:
www.chriskeniston.com/newsletter.html

Questions? Comments?
I would love to hear from you! You can reach me at:
chris@chriskeniston.com

www.ingramcontent.com/pod-product-compliance
Lightning Source LLC
Chambersburg PA
CBHW031056310726
48969CB00007B/2298